Reid glanced at Megan.

From the very start she had struck him as unusual and intriguing. He wanted more from her than friendship, yet he wasn't after a casual affair, either. Sex with no commitment or deep feeling didn't interest him. He frowned slightly as he tried to figure out exactly what he *did* want from her.

Megan's nerves seemed attuned to Reid's slightest movement. She wanted him to take her hand, but after the way she had pulled back before, she knew he wouldn't reach out again. Nor did she feel confident enough to reach out to him. She tried to keep from sighing in frustration. He was all any woman could dream of in a man: handsome, successful, companionable, incredibly sexy. So why did she feel this fear?

Dear Reader,

Spellbinders! That's what we're striving for. The editors at Silhouette are determined to capture your imagination and win your heart with every single book we publish. Each month, six Special Editions are chosen with *you* in mind.

Our authors are our inspiration. Writers such as Nora Roberts, Tracy Sinclair, Kathleen Eagle, Carole Halston and Linda Howard—to name but a few—are masters at creating endearing characters and heartrending love stories. Their characters are everyday people—just like you and me—whose lives have been touched by love, whose dreams and desires suddenly come true!

So find a cozy, quiet place to read, and create your own special moment with a Silhouette Special Edition.

Sincerely,

The Editors
SILHOUETTE BOOKS

LYNDA TRENT
A Certain Smile

Silhouette Special Edition

Published by Silhouette Books New York

America's Publisher of Contemporary Romance

To Nick Rowe,
who has always been there
when the chips were down.

SILHOUETTE BOOKS
300 East 42nd St., New York, N.Y. 10017

ISBN: 0-373-09409-4

First Silhouette Books printing October 1987

America's Publisher of Contemporary Romance

Printed in the U.S.A.

Books by Lynda Trent

Silhouette Intimate Moments

Designs #36
Taking Chances #68
Castles in the Sand #134

Silhouette Desire

The Enchantment #201
Simple Pleasures #223

Silhouette Special Edition

High Society #378
A Certain Smile #409

LYNDA TRENT

started writing romances at the insistence of a friend, but it was her husband who provided moral support whenever her resolve flagged. Now husband and wife are both full-time writers, and despite the ups and downs of this demanding career, they love every— well, *almost* every—minute of it.

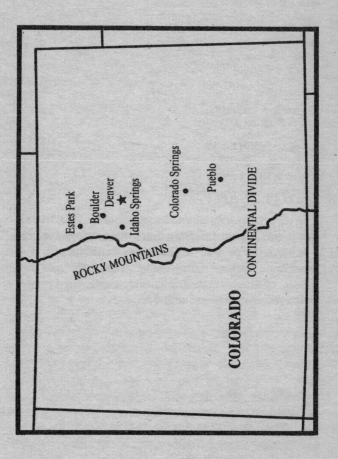

Chapter One

Megan Wayne looked up from the magazine she held in her lap as the door to the inner office opened. A tall, impeccably dressed man with silver hair and broad shoulders emerged and said to the secretary, "Cancel my afternoon appointments, Miss Bain. Something has come up."

The secretary glanced at Megan, who was already rising to her feet. "Excuse me, Mr. Spencer, but I'm here for our appointment, and I've waited thirty minutes as it is."

Reid Spencer turned, and Megan found herself gazing at what had to be the most handsome man she had ever seen. Though she had featured him in an article the year before, this was her first face-to-face encounter with the owner of the While-Away sporting-goods line. Despite his thick silver hair, she knew he was no older than forty. She hadn't expected his eyes to be so deep a blue; she certainly hadn't anticipated that his face and form could trigger such an immediate response in her.

"I'm sorry, Ms. Wayne. You are Ms. Wayne, I assume?" he said in a smooth, commanding baritone.

Megan nodded and stepped closer. Even though the man was frowning at her, he positively exuded charisma. Nonetheless, business was business, and she summoned up her most assertive tone. "I made this appointment a month ago. You've put off seeing me twice. This article is commissioned work. I'm afraid I must insist on keeping our appointment today."

"I hope you realize I haven't been avoiding you just to be difficult. However, I—"

"No?" she interrupted. The resonance in his deep voice touched a part of her that she thought had been numbed forever. Although the sensation was unsettling, she was determined to get her interview done. "Then why have you?"

A muscle knotted in Reid's lean jaw, but he forced his lips to smile. "By all means, come in, Ms. Wayne. I'll give you ten minutes."

"Thanks," she said wryly.

She followed him into his office and took one of the leather chairs in front of the massive oak desk. The office was decorated in maroon and cream with navy accents, the epitome of masculine elegance. Reid lowered his lithe frame into the tufted leather swivel chair behind the desk, glanced at his Rolex and then looked directly at her as he waited for her to begin.

The shyness she had worked so long and hard to overcome welled up under his hypnotic gaze. For a moment Megan hesitated, then flipped open her notepad and tried to look professional. "As you know, I'm a free-lance writer, and I'm doing this article on you for *Success Un-*

limited magazine. The angle I'm going for is how rapidly you've attained your phenomenal success with your sporting-goods equipment."

"Yes, Ms. Wayne, I know exactly who you are." His voice was cool, reserved, but his aloofness didn't mask its rich timbre. "You wrote an article about one of my products last year, and, as a result, my sales suffered considerably."

Megan's hazel eyes widened in surprise. "I didn't expect you to remember."

"I always remember events that affect my business. Especially when the results are both negative and uncalled for."

"The heater didn't work properly," she protested. "The article was a comparison guide for people interested in purchasing camping equipment. I tried the heater, and it didn't work as well as your competitor's."

"Ms. Wayne, I employ a number of highly skilled engineers in my products-development department, and they have assured me that the heater performs exactly as it should."

"Perhaps they should take it up into the mountains and give it a try. I couldn't get it to heat up the tent."

Reid leaned forward and fixed her with an imperious stare. The air fairly crackled with tension. "The heater works!"

Undaunted, Megan, too, leaned forward. "I would have frozen if I hadn't also brought along the other brand." Realizing that this interview wasn't going the way she had planned, she sat back and drew a calming breath before continuing. "The questions I want to ask you have to do with your success, not your catalytic heater. Two years ago you owned a sporting-goods store here in Boulder and were experimenting with the development of your own line of equipment. Now you have a large manufacturing facility here, and you own stores in Denver, Colorado Springs and Pueblo that sell only your line of equipment. Some say you will soon be a reckoning factor for the big national lines to consider. What caused this meteoric climb?''

"Hard work and excellent products. Products that function properly.'' He glared at her as if he wished she would go away. A light began flashing on his phone. "Excuse me,'' he said as he answered it.

Megan sighed. She could feel the minutes ticking away. At this rate she would never finish the interview, and she had already sold the idea to the magazine. Not only would it be a step up in her career to be published by the national magazine, but she had already planned how she would spend the money.

As she watched, Reid's stern expression softened slightly and a faint smile tilted the corners of his mouth. "Terry. What's up, honey?'' Even his voice was gentler. Megan wondered who this Terry was. She was almost positive Reid Spencer was divorced.

Reid extended his arm to bring his wristwatch from under his suit sleeve. "No, I can't do that. I have a full schedule today. Besides, that's not my responsibility. You know that. No, Terry, I don't want to talk to her. I'm busy.'' The tender look disappeared as he said, "Hello, Pamela. No, I won't come over and fix your television. No. Because the endless odd jobs quit when the marriage did.'' There was a pause, and Reid's face grew stony as he listened. Megan could faintly hear the feminine voice of the caller, but she looked away as if she hadn't heard either side of the obviously personal conversation Spencer was having with his ex-wife.

"If the television is broken, call a repairman. You can afford it. Pamela, don't... Hello, Jeanette. Yes, baby, I know the Madonna special is on tonight. Have your mother call a repairman. What do you mean, she doesn't know how? That's ridiculous." He rubbed his eyes tiredly. "Yes, she can. If the repairman can't fix it today, you and Terry can come to my house to watch TV. Sure, baby. Any time." The soft note was back in his voice as he told his daughter goodbye and hung up.

"Sorry about that," he said to Megan. "I forgot to tell Miss Bain to hold the calls."

"That's all right. Now, about this almost overnight success..."

Again a light on the phone flashed, and Reid shrugged apologetically as he picked up the receiver. "Right, Johnson. I'm on my way. I'll meet you at the lab." He hung up and stood. "I'm sorry, Ms. Wayne, but I've run out of time. Why don't you check with Miss Bain and set up another time."

"What? I can't believe this! You didn't even give me ten minutes!"

"I'm late for a meeting, as you just heard. Miss Bain is new, and she overbooked this afternoon. The meeting at the lab is one I can't miss. I'm sorry." He came around the desk and held out his hand.

Automatically Megan took it. The warm pressure of his strong fingers sent a tingle up her arm, and her lips parted in surprise. Their eyes met and held. She could see silver flecks in his eyes, and she had the sudden, curious sensation of knowing him on some deep, elemental level.

Reid couldn't look away, either. Megan Wayne's honey-green eyes had a sensuous, bedroom hint in their depths. He'd found them stirring and disturbing during the entire interview. Her skin was flawless and creamy, and she wore very little makeup. Although he judged her to be in her late thirties, there was an elfin quality about her. Perpetual youth, he mused, as if she lived life to its fullest every moment of the day.

Suddenly Reid realized he was staring, and he released her delicate hand. In the most businesslike tone he could command, he said, "Please arrange another time with Miss Bain."

"But . . ." Megan attempted to stop him, but Reid was already out the door, striding past his secretary.

"Do you want another appointment?" Miss Bain asked as Megan walked to her desk. "He has an opening next month on the fifteenth."

"Next month! The article is due in a week."

"I'm sorry, but that's the best I can do."

Megan shook her head slowly. "Never mind, Miss Bain. I'll think of something else."

Megan left the office building and walked to her car. Although it was only September, there was a frosty nip in the air. The foothills of the Rocky Mountains were mounded in brilliant fall foliage beyond the outskirts of Boulder, and an early winter seemed likely.

Megan started her car and drove out of the parking lot onto Broadway. One way or another, she was determined to get the interview—not just for the money, though she could definitely use it, but because now it had become a challenge.

She drove to her house, a small peach-colored Victorian with white gingerbread and federal-blue shutters, and parked in the garage at the back. The two-story house was too large for her now that she was alone, but she loved it nevertheless. Fond memories of her marriage were lodged here. She could recall the afternoon Hugh had planted the maple at the edge of the patio.

Those had been happy days, the days before multiple sclerosis became a personal thing and not just a fund-raising drive on television. Now Hugh was dead, and Megan was left alone in the house they had planned to fill with children.

Unlocking the back door, she entered her spacious kitchen. Like the outside shutters, the kitchen was painted a restful shade of deep blue, which was repeated in the tiny flowers in the accent panels of wallpaper. Megan put her purse and keys on the oak breakfast table and sat down to think. She was rarely dissuaded from anything she had her mind firmly set to do, and she was determined to interview Reid Spencer.

Spencer was something of an enigma. She should dislike him for his condescending attitude toward her and his rudeness at not keeping his appointment, but she didn't feel that way at all. Nothing about him was as she had thought it would be. The grainy, black-and-white photos of him that often appeared in the local newspaper hadn't begun to do him justice. Eyes like his could never be captured on film, and she had assumed his hair was blond, not prematurely silver. Nothing could have prepared her for the sensual baritone of his voice.

She shook her head to get her thoughts back on track. She was after an interview, not the man himself. Her gaze fell on the phone book, and she smiled. Ruffling through the pages, she found the S listings. She ran her finger down the page, not really daring to hope that he might have a home number listed. But his name seemed to leap off the page at her. His address was given as 132 Juniper. Megan's smile broadened. That was only four blocks away! Humming a merry tune, Megan closed the phone book and prepared to wait until quitting time.

Reid was relieved when Johnson finally completed his report on the new insulating foam-and-seal design for the ice chests. Johnson was thorough and efficient, but he spoke in a drawling monotone that no one could listen to attentively for more than ten minutes. The review had lasted more than an hour. Everything seemed to be as it should be, so Reid gave his approval for fabrication of the prototype ice chests.

Glancing at the brushed gold face of his watch, Reid closed the meeting and reached for the wall phone. Quickly he punched in Pamela's number. Jeanette answered on the first ring, and Reid smiled at the thought that she was never very far from the phone. "Hi, baby," he said. "Are you and Terry coming over to watch television tonight?"

"No, Dad. Our set is working now. I just hit it with my hand a couple of times, and it came back on."

Reid felt a twinge of disappointment. He had hoped the girls would drop by. The only thing he regretted about divorcing Pamela was not being able to see his daughters every day. "Did Terry get her learner's permit?"

"Yes, but she can't drive alone until she gets her real license. I'll sure be glad when *I* can drive. I hate being fifteen."

Reid smiled. "Time will pass before you know it."

"Is it all right if Terry and I come over this weekend?"

"Of course. Bring your tennis rackets, and we'll play a few sets."

"All right. I have to go now. Terry says she's expecting a call from that creepy Billy Madison."

Reid heard a muffled thud and a giggle from Jeanette. "I gather Terry overheard that?"

"Sure. She's sitting right here. We'll see you Saturday, Dad. Bye."

Reid said goodbye and hung up. He missed his daughters' teasing as much as he missed being a full-time father. However, he didn't miss being Pamela's husband at all. That had been a more than full-time job. That business earlier about the broken television set was only a small example. Pamela needed to be taken care of constantly. When she had unexpectedly asked for a divorce two years earlier, he couldn't have been more amazed. Their marriage had not been based on deep and passionate love, but he had thought she was happy right up to the day she left with the accountant from the bank.

Reid hadn't contested the divorce, but he did try to get custody of his girls. Despite his arguments that he was the better parent, the judge gave custody to Pamela. Reid had been bitter, but because Pamela allowed him almost unrestricted visitation rights with the girls, he had adjusted. Her new marriage had ended several months before, and now she was trying her best to maneuver herself back into a remarriage with Reid. He had no intention of making the same mistake twice. Not even for his daughters.

Reid drove to his apartment and let himself in. He was basically neat, and with only one person to make a mess, the apartment stayed fairly clean. He loosened his tie as he went through the day's mail, putting the bills in a cubbyhole on his desk and tossing the junk mail into the trash.

He went up the narrow stairs to his bedroom and quickly shed his tailored suit. When he wasn't in the office, Reid believed in relaxing. Like everything else he did, he worked very hard at it. He dressed in jeans and a loose red sweater, then pulled on scruffy tennis shoes over his sweat socks.

As he hung up his suit, he thought about the woman he had met that afternoon. She hadn't been the most beautiful woman he had ever seen, but she was easily the most intriguing. He recalled the golden lights in her green eyes, and the way they tilted just a bit to make her casual glance so captivating. Her voice had been soft and musical with a faint southern accent, and she looked as though she smiled more often than she frowned. She also appeared to be very capable. After Pamela, he liked that in a woman. What was her first name? Margo? Meg? No, Megan. That was it. Megan Wayne. He wondered if she was married and decided she must be, though at the time he hadn't thought to notice if she was wearing a wedding ring.

He went downstairs and into the kitchen to get a steak out of the refrigerator. It was a larger piece of meat than he could eat, but shopping for one was difficult. He decided to cook it all and save what he didn't eat for the next day.

As he was unwrapping the meat, he looked out his window. Each unit of the apartment complex had a small yard, and he enjoyed a clear view of the park across the street. At the edge of his patio was a new gas grill, which had been installed a few days earlier, and tonight he was going to cook his first meal on it. Reid salted and peppered the raw meat, put a potato into the microwave, gathered the brochures for the grill and went out back.

He set the meat plate on the picnic table and sat down to read the instructions. Soon he realized he would need all his engineering training to figure them out. Somehow it hadn't seemed so difficult in the store. Now he read that before its first use the grill had to be seasoned. Reid slouched down in the redwood chair, crossed one ankle over the opposite knee and proceeded to reread the confusing instructions.

"Hello, there."

Reid glanced up to see a woman jogging toward him across his yard. On second look he recognized her as Megan Wayne. She had on a pink warm-up suit, and her shoulder-length hair was pulled back beneath a pink sweatband. Dressed so brightly and casually, she looked younger than she had in his office. "Hello," he finally said.

"I hope you don't mind my stopping by. I happened to be out jogging and saw you sitting here."

"I've never noticed you around here before. Do you live nearby?"

"I live on Appletree. Usually I run at the track around the football field. Do you jog?"

"No."

"What do you do for entertainment?"

"Ms. Wayne, if this is an interview..."

"I was merely being sociable. I was going to work up to an interview later." She smiled, and he felt his world tilt.

"You're certainly persistent." He wondered if her gleaming chestnut hair was as soft as it looked. And her skin. She seemed to glow from within.

"I am when it comes to an interview. It's the way I make my living."

"Then there's no Mr. Wayne?"

"Not anymore."

"Divorced?"

"Widowed. Multiple sclerosis. He died three years ago."

"I'm sorry to hear that."

"Thank you. I understand you're divorced?"

"That's right." Here it comes, he thought. The bait-and-hook routine. For two years Reid had successfully angled his way around women who found his wealth too attractive to pass up.

"That's too bad. Were those your daughters on the phone this afternoon?"

"Yes," he said simply. At her inquisitive look he added, "Terry is seventeen, Jeanette is fifteen."

"That's the one thing I regret—not having children, I mean. But it just didn't work out. Is that a new grill?"

"Yes." If she was flirting with him, her technique was certainly subtle.

"I have the same brand. Do you like it?"

"I've never used it." He waved the papers he was holding. "I'm still reading the instructions."

"I threw mine away. They were impossible to understand."

"It says here that the grill must be properly seasoned, but it doesn't say how to do it. According to this, it's very important."

"Just brush a little corn oil on it, and light the burner."

"Maybe that's why you had trouble with my catalytic heater. Instructions are meant to be followed."

"I did follow your instructions. The thing didn't work."

Reid refrained from comment and went back to reading the brochure.

"These are nice apartments. Do you like it here?"

"Yes. Ordinarily they're very private," he said pointedly.

"I live in a house. I'm not sure I'd like an apartment. I need space around me. Have you always lived in Boulder?"

"No, I grew up in Denver. Ms. Wayne, if you were jogging, I wouldn't want to keep you."

"No problem. And call me Megan. Ms. Wayne sounds so stuffy." Again she smiled, and he looked away quickly. What was it about her that threatened to melt his reserve so easily?

To cover his confusion, Reid got up and went to the barbecue grill. None of the knobs seemed to be quite like those pictured in the booklet. "I think I have the wrong instructions," he said with a frown.

Megan came over and knelt down. "This is just like mine. Brush oil on the grill. Then turn this knob all the way on, and it will make a clicking sound. Once it ignites the gas, turn it down to cooking level."

"That's not what it says here."

"Maybe not, but that's how it works." She gazed into his eyes and asked, "Was your father in the sporting-goods business?"

"Why do you want to know?"

"I didn't realize it was a secret."

"Why could you possibly care what my father did for a living?"

"This is that interview I told you I was going to work into the conversation."

"Oh." Somehow he was disappointed. On one level he had hoped she really was flirting with him.

"Why did you think I was asking all these personal questions?"

"Well, I thought you might be... That is, you could have been..."

"You thought this was a come-on?" she exclaimed. "That's it, isn't it!"

"You don't have to make it sound so unbelievable. Women have been known to flirt with me before."

"Well, that's really something!" she snapped. His accusation had hit closer to home than she wanted to admit. Megan never wore her new sweat suit to jog around the football track, nor did she wear makeup to impress other joggers. With a jolt she realized she *had* been flirting. "I can't believe you thought that," she bluffed.

"I'm sorry."

"You think I ran all the way over here to flirt with you? Incredible!" She was trying hard to remember anyone else she had gone to such lengths to interview. There had been no one.

"I said I'm sorry. Why are you making such a federal case out of it?" He stood up and frowned at her.

Megan got to her feet and bit her lower lip before she finally said, "Because I think you may be right, and I don't want to admit it."

Reid blinked. "Good Lord, but you're honest!"

"I know. Subtlety isn't my strong point."

"Was this afternoon's interview on the level?"

"Of course! Do you think I have nothing better to do than make appointments with strangers and pretend to interview them in order to flirt?"

"I think you're the most confusing woman I've ever met."

"This isn't going the way I planned it," she muttered. "I guess I'll write another article instead."

"Isn't this one already sold?"

"Yes, but that's okay." She turned to go.

"Wait a minute. Don't be so hasty. I'm flattered you want to do an article on me. *Success Unlimited* is an important publication."

She looked at him over her shoulder. "Then you'll give me an interview?"

"I'll do better than that. I'll share my steak with you, and we can talk over dinner. Unless you have other plans," he added quickly.

"No, no. I have nothing else planned for tonight."

"Good. I'll put another potato in the microwave. You read this booklet and see if you can figure out the instructions."

When he came back out, Megan shut the booklet and said, "I was right. Where's your cooking oil?"

Reid brought out a bottle of oil and a pastry brush. "Where does it say how to do it?" He was thumbing through the brochure again.

"In there toward the back," she lied as she took the oil and brush. In no time she had the grill going.

"I still don't see it," he said as he laid the booklet aside. He put the steak on to cook and carefully turned the dial to eight.

"That's too hot. You'll burn the meat."

"Nope. I did find the page that says how to cook steak. Trust me. I know what I'm doing."

As they were finishing dinner, Megan said, "Quit moping. It wasn't *that* burned."

"Shoe leather would have been more tender," he grumbled.

"Cooking outside just takes practice. Next time I'll have you over to my house and show you how my grill works."

"I thought you said they were identical."

"They are. I'm being subtle." She gave him her disarming smile.

"Let's go into the living room, where we'll be more comfortable." He showed her the way and turned on the stereo, filling the room with soft music.

Megan sat on the plump couch and looked around in approval. As in his office, the walls were cream-colored, but here the furniture was forest green and the carpet a rich gold. "You have wonderful taste. Or did you use a decorator?"

"No, no decorator. I know what I like."

She ran her finger over the sensuous curve of a large crystal sculpture. The warm glow of a lamp made the room as cozy as it was elegant. Through the large window she saw the sun setting over the rolling foothills. "I didn't intend to stay so long. It's getting dark."

"I'll drive you home."

"I'm not afraid to walk," she said decisively. "Of course, I didn't bring a coat, and the evenings *are* cold," she added.

Reid sat beside her and pivoted to face her. "So. Go ahead and ask your questions. What else do you want to know about me?"

Everything, she thought as the lamplight gilded his strong features and accented his muscular body. She cleared her throat. "What sort of background are you from?"

"Blue collar," he said easily. "My father worked in a garage in Denver. My mother was a sales clerk. They're both dead now. What about you?"

"My father is an English professor at Queens College in Charlotte, North Carolina. My mother has always been a housewife."

"North Carolina. So that's where the accent is from. I wondered."

"I didn't know it still showed. I've lived in Colorado for years."

"I like it."

Megan found herself drowning in the blue depths of his eyes and not caring at all to save herself. With a start she looked away and promptly launched the next interview question. "When did you decide to become a success? I've never talked with anyone successful who didn't make the conscious decision to be so."

"Very perceptive. In high school I decided that I wanted more from life than breaking my back in someone else's garage. I did whatever it took to go to college and get an engineering degree. I saved every extra penny I could, and when I had a chance to buy a partnership in a sporting-goods store, I knew it was a sound business venture, and I did it. We were successful, and later I bought out my partner. By then I was getting good feedback on my ideas for developing a new line of camping equipment. I started small but kept at it until about a year and a half ago. That's when I got my big break and started producing my own line."

"After your divorce?" she asked quietly. Reid made it all sound so simple, but Megan suspected that his efforts had been gargantuan, his determination unswerving and the sacrifices heavy ones.

"About two months after the divorce was final." He studied her features in the lamp's soft glow. "Shouldn't you be writing this down?"

"I have an unusually good memory." She doubted she would ever forget anything this compelling man said. "So you've realized all your goals but one."

"Which one?"

"You're still working harder than anyone I've ever tried to interview. It took me a month to get in, I was put off twice and Miss Bain said your next opening is a month from now. By my definition, that's working hard."

"I guess I keep long hours, but I enjoy my work."

"You must be a type-A personality. My guess is that you thrive on work."

"So my ex-wife used to tell me," he said lightly. "What's wrong with that?"

"Nothing, I suppose. What do you do for fun?"

"I play tennis, for one thing. As a matter of fact, my girls and I are playing this weekend."

"You against the two of them, I'll bet." She laughed. "Thriving on competition once again."

"What do you do to have fun?" he asked testily.

"I go for walks in the woods, have picnics—things like that. Would you like to go on one with me?"

"A picnic? At this time of year?"

"Wear warm clothes. How about tomorrow?"

"A picnic?" he repeated. "I haven't been on a picnic in years. Not since I was a boy, in fact."

"Then it's time you did. I'll pick you up tomorrow." She smiled as she stood up. "I'd better be going. Thanks for dinner. And for the interview."

"Wait. I said I'd drive you home."

"No need to do that. The streets are well-lit, and if I run, I won't get too cold." As she talked she walked briskly through the kitchen. "I'll see you tomorrow." As she trotted out into the night she called back, "Okay if I call you Reid?"

"Sure. I thought you already did." He watched as she waved and jogged out of sight. He wasn't accustomed to women who saw themselves home. He liked that.

Chapter Two

Megan spent the day typing up her interview for *Success Unlimited*. A lengthy call to Reid's new but already well-informed secretary filled in the gaps of how the business worked and the range of products While-Away handled. To round her story off, she interviewed the manager of the local While-Away sporting-goods store, a man who had worked for Reid for years. By the time Reid was off work, Megan had her article finished and in the mail.

She dressed in her favorite soft, snug jeans, and pulled a bulky yellow sweater over a striped cotton shirt. After slipping on her jacket, she gathered the food and blanket and turned on a light in the kitchen in the event she didn't get back before dark.

Reid was ready when she arrived and was on his way out to the car before she had time to go to his door. As she watched him moving toward her with long, self-assured strides, she became aware that every time she saw him, he looked better than the time before. His deep blue sweater made his eyes look the shade of an evening sky, and his surprising silver hair rippled in the breeze.

"This is crazy," he said by way of a greeting. "You know that?"

"No, it's not. We'll have fun. Get in."

He got in on the passenger side with the barely concealed reluctance of a man who prefers to drive. Megan pretended not to notice. "I thought we'd go up into the foothills. There's not enough time to reach the mountains before dark."

She was a skillful driver, and Reid seemed to have relaxed a bit by the time she parked in a deserted picnic area in a wooded thicket.

"No one else is here. What luck!" she exclaimed.

"Everyone else is home by the fire," he grumbled.

"What sissies." She opened the trunk and bent over to get the picnic basket.

Reid grinned at the sight of her rounded buttocks in the tight jeans. Clearly, she had attributes he hadn't had time to notice before. He took the heavy basket from her, and she tossed the quilt over her shoulder.

"Let's go over there under that tree."

"But the picnic tables are over here."

"Tables are for houses. Picnic dinners are meant to be eaten on the ground." She popped the quilt in the air and let it billow out over the dry grass. She sat on it crosslegged and motioned for him to join her.

Reid lowered his body onto the quilt and shifted to avoid a handful of pebbles beneath the fabric.

"I hope you like tuna salad. I worked all day and didn't have time to fix anything fancy." She took the lid off a container of deviled eggs as Reid opened a bag of chips. "If you expect to get any food, you'll have to work fast. I could eat a horse, neigh and all."

Reid grinned. Very few women in his experience admitted to having an appetite at all. He took a bite of sandwich and nodded his approval. "Magnificent. My compliments to the chef."

"Thanks, but it's hard to go wrong with tuna."

Drawing a deep breath, he said, "I'd forgotten how the woods smell in the autumn."

She nodded. "It's a totally different scent than at any other time of year. Most people don't even notice that."

"Most people don't see it as close as we are," he said in mock complaint.

She looked at him and smiled. "Admit it. This is fun."

"It's relaxing. I am enjoying myself," he said.

"Why were you so elusive when I tried to talk to you in your office? Were you honestly that offended by my article on the catalytic heater?"

"I was pretty upset at the time. The article appeared the week I was putting through an important deal with a chain of discount stores, and it could have cost me quite a bit of business."

"I had no intention of doing that. I was merely reporting matters as I found them."

"The deal went through. Apparently I was more convincing than your article. Besides, the heater has never been one of my biggest sales items."

"Ever ask yourself why?" She looked at him with feigned innocence as she ate a deviled egg.

"Don't start on that again. The heater works."

"Have it your way."

Reid studied her as she ate. She had an effortless ease about her whether she was in the woods or in his office. With her tight jeans and floppy sweater she looked young. "How old are you?" he was surprised to find himself saying.

"Thirty-nine. How old are you? Never mind, I already know. You're forty."

"How did you know that?"

"I researched you. For my article, I mean," she added hastily.

"You look younger than thirty-nine."

"Thanks, but age never has meant much to me. I haven't felt a day older since I was about fifteen. I hope I act more mature, but inside I'm the same." She spread her arms as if to embrace the world and said impulsively, "There's so much I want to see and do."

"Does remarrying fall into that category?"

"No way. I was happily married to Hugh for twelve years, but it's not something I want to repeat."

"It must have been difficult for you to lose him."

"You can't imagine. I structured my entire life around him. I chose to do that, and I don't regret it, but in a way it made the end more difficult. When we discovered he was ill, I began writing to supplement his disability income. After... well, with no office to go to, for weeks I would find myself listening to see if he needed something or walking into his room to check up on him."

"Separate bedrooms?"

"He preferred it that way toward the end. He had trouble sleeping and needed the quiet." Megan gazed pensively at the forest. "I didn't mind giving up my more active pursuits. Not really. After all, being with Hugh was certainly more important than horseback riding or backpacking. I knew that one day he would be gone, while the mountains are forever. It's a matter of priorities."

"I understand. That still doesn't explain why you don't want to remarry. Did you love him that much?"

Megan was silent a long time, and Reid was about to apologize for being too personal when she said, "Our love wasn't the kind you're thinking of. It wasn't all fireworks and glory. It was steady and deep, and it would have lasted, but we weren't what some romantic types would call soul mates. Marriage requires a great deal of work. In being married, a person has to give up something to get something in return. I had companionship, warmth, stability, security—at least in the beginning."

"What did you give up to get them?" Reid asked quietly.

"My freedom." Megan shook her head briskly. "No, I didn't mean that. Forget I said it."

Reid reached across the quilt and covered her hand with his. Megan grew very still. "There's nothing wrong with saying that. With an invalid husband to care for, I'd be more amazed if you had been able to keep your freedom."

"I don't mind. I never minded it." When Reid was silent, she looked at him defensively. "Well, I *didn't*."

"I believe you."

He didn't sound convinced, and worse than that, she wasn't so sure she believed it herself. At the time she had been sure, but now, well, she was enjoying her freedom more than she had ever expected. And she was feeling irrationally guilty about it. She decided to turn the tables. "What about you? Are you planning to remarry?"

"Absolutely not. I'm not good marriage material."

"No? Why not?" She leaned forward curiously. "Do you have some strange quirk I'm not aware of?"

"Of course not. I just enjoy my work too well. There's no extra time to cultivate a marriage."

"You find time for your daughters."

"That's different. Terry and Jeanette aren't demanding."

"They sound nice. Do they look like you?" she asked easily.

"Jeanette does, a little. Only her hair is still dark, of course. Terry looks like her mother. Would you like to meet them sometime?"

"That would be nice."

"They'll be over Saturday. Do you play tennis? Maybe you'd like to join us."

"Sounds like fun. You know," she mused, "this is the perfect way to start a relationship." At his startled look she explained, "You know that I don't have marriage in mind, and I know you don't, either. Ergo, no muss, no fuss. We can just be friends, without all the usual man-woman confusion. Don't you agree?"

He seemed to hesitate, then finally said, "You're probably right. We won't have to play some ridiculous parlor game of constantly sidestepping to prevent the other from getting too emotionally involved."

"Right. Although that's not likely to happen. Not with both of us so happy with our free and unfettered state."

Reid nodded, but he somehow wished she hadn't been quite so adamant that she could never become emotionally involved with him. Megan was an attractive woman, and he wasn't certain he wanted no involvement at all.

Megan reached for a bag of cookies in the bottom of the picnic basket and wondered why Reid was so sure he wouldn't fall for her. She was no femme fatale, but she wasn't a dog either. "Cookie?" she asked to cover her mixed emotions. "It's an old family recipe."

He watched her open the bag. "What recipe? Those are store-bought cookies."

"I didn't say it was *my* family recipe. Actually, these are exactly like the ones Mom gave me. She isn't fond of cooking."

"You know, it's hard to believe that we met only yesterday, and here we are, freezing our buns off on a picnic, agreeing not to fall in love and sharing cookies like your Mom didn't make."

"Is that what we agreed?" she asked in surprise. "Not to fall in love?"

He gazed into her eyes and found himself unable to look away. Deep in their forest-hued depths lurked... what? A forgotten memory? A promise not yet formed? "It's as if I knew you before," he murmured, "even though I know that's not possible."

"Could we have met somewhere and forgotten it? A party perhaps?" she asked faintly.

"No." His voice was soft and sensuous as his eyes searched her face. "I would have remembered you."

"It's getting late," she forced herself to say. "In no time it'll be dark."

Reluctantly Reid looked away. The sky was indeed darkening fast. In the hills twilight was fleeting. "Right. Let's gather up all this stuff while we can still find our way around."

He put the leftovers and containers into the basket while Megan dumped the trash in a covered barrel. Both reached for the basket at the same time. "I can carry it," she said.

"I already have it."

"So do I." She frowned at him stubbornly. "You aren't trying to give me the little-lady routine, are you?"

"Have it your way," he answered with a shrug.

"I just can't stand being treated like a hothouse flower," she continued. "I'm as capable of carrying a picnic basket as you are."

"Anything you say, pal."

Megan smiled. "I guess I do get carried away at times. It's just that I've taken care of myself for so long that I'm not accustomed to having someone carry things for me."

"Freedom is carrying your own picnic basket," Reid replied sagely.

"Get in the car," she said with a grimace.

By the time they returned to Boulder, night had fallen and a sliver of a moon hung over the black hulk of the mountains. Megan parked in front of Reid's apartment and asked, "Tell me honestly, did you enjoy the picnic?"

"Yes, I did. Why don't you come inside and warm up?"

Megan hesitated. She was very tempted to do just that, but she couldn't let herself. Reid was like a lodestone to her, and as it was she had to struggle to keep her distance. When she'd said she didn't intend to get emotionally involved with a man, to remarry, she had said the words by rote, just as she had long thought them to herself. On hearing them, however, she'd wondered if they truly reflected the way she felt now. Certainly Reid had jumped to agree with her. If he was as adamant as he sounded about remaining unencumbered, she had better strive harder to keep her emotional distance. Despite his initial aloofness and somewhat intimidating elegance, his gorgeous body and straightforward manner combined to endow him with more raw sex appeal than any man she had ever seen. Against her will, she found him almost irresistible.

"Well?"

"Uh...no, thanks. I need to get home. Some other time, perhaps."

Reid looked disappointed, but he nodded. "The offer is open. So, will I see you Saturday? How about three o'clock at the courts across the street?"

"I'll be there."

For a heart-stopping moment she thought he was about to lean over and kiss her, and her lips involuntarily parted. Then he opened the car door, got out and waved. Megan watched him unlock his door and reach in to snap on the lights. What was there about this particular man that seemed to tumble her thoughts into chaos? She didn't believe in love at first sight. Besides, they had agreed not to fall in love at all. Slowly she pulled away from the curb and drove home.

Saturday Megan again dressed in her pink warm-up suit and rummaged through her storage closet in search of her tennis racket. She hadn't played in quite a while, but she had been fairly good at the sport at one time. If Reid proved to be as fond of tennis as he'd indicated, she could improve her skills quickly.

Experimentally she swung the racket in the air. In college she had made the varsity team, and they had won the state meet. She was looking forward to playing again. She tied her hair into a ponytail to keep it out of her eyes, grabbed her purse and, without stopping to analyze her motives further, almost skipped in her eagerness to meet Reid and his daughters.

She walked over the grass toward the tennis courts. Even from a distance it was easy to spot the impressive-looking man in pristine tennis whites vying with two bouncy teenage girls. Megan hung back for a minute and watched them. Despite the fact that the girls were running him all over the court with their alternate shots, Reid was doing an admirable job of returning their volleys.

Both girls had dark brown hair and Reid's trim, lithe build. The taller wore colorful sweatbands on her wrists and forehead and was dressed in a fluorescent yellow outfit, very similar in color to the tennis balls. The slightly smaller girl wore jeans and a sweatshirt. She had Germanic features like her father, whereas the other girl's face was more delicate. Both had Reid's firm jaw, and from the competitive spirit they were displaying, Megan suspected they were all equally stubborn.

The smaller girl sent the ball into the net, and Reid chortled triumphantly. "I won!"

"Jeanette, you should have aimed higher," Terry scolded good-naturedly. "Dad, next time she plays on your side."

"Terry's just mad because there aren't any boys playing today," Jeanette retorted with a grin. "When there are, she bats half the balls into their court so she'll have to go get them. Right, Dad?" She dodged behind Reid as Terry swatted at her in pretended outrage.

Megan smiled. They made a lovely family. She had always regretted having no brothers or sisters to spar with in a friendly way. She could see why Reid was so fond of the girls; they obviously doted on him. Jeanette had slipped her hand into his, and Terry was animatedly telling him about something that had happened in school the day before. Terry was already showing signs of the classic beauty she would soon become. And although Jeanette was still rounded, midway between puberty and maturity, her beauty, too, was beginning to emerge. Reid had every reason to be proud of his healthy, attractive and obviously spirited daughters.

Megan walked closer, and when Reid saw her, his face lit with a smile. "Girls, I want you to meet a friend of mine, Megan Wayne. Megan, this is Terry, and this is Jeanette."

"Hello," Megan said. "I've been looking forward to meeting you."

At once the smiles faded from the girls' faces. Jeanette gave Megan and her tennis racket a level, appraising look, then turned away. Terry said coolly, "Dad didn't tell us anything about you."

As though Reid were oblivious to Terry's slight, he said to her, "Well, I haven't known Megan very long. She's a free-lance writer for magazines."

"Oh," Terry responded with great indifference.

"Can we play another game, Dad?" Jeanette asked.

"You and Terry play. I need time to catch my breath."

Jeanette again perused Megan. To her father she said, "You never got tired before after only one game."

"Terry was just telling me that she's going to be in her class play," Reid said to Megan. Terry glared at him as if he had betrayed her deepest secret.

"Oh? Which play are you doing?"

"*Oklahoma!*"

"Really? I was in *Oklahoma!* in my senior year of high school."

Terry looked as if she seriously doubted it.

"I played Ado Annie," Megan said lamely.

"I'm the lead," Terry replied.

Megan's smile faltered. Terry was obviously hostile, though Reid didn't seem to notice. She turned her attention to Jeanette. "Are you in the play, too?"

"It's just for juniors and seniors. I'm a sophomore. We don't get to do anything."

"Perhaps next year..."

"Nope. Terry is the actress. I don't care about things like that. I'd rather ride horses."

"You ride?" Megan said in relief, finding a common ground at last. "So do I."

"Do you ride English?"

"No, Western."

"Oh. I ride English." To Reid she said, "Are you rested yet? Let's play."

"Sure," he said heartily. "Let's all play. You and I against Terry and Megan."

"What!" Terry demanded.

"I . . . I'm afraid I can't play today," Megan said hurriedly. "Some other time maybe."

"But you came all the way over to play," Reid objected.

"You asked someone over on *our* weekend?" Terry exclaimed.

"If she isn't going to play tennis, why is she carrying that racket around?" Jeanette asked no one in particular.

Megan looked at her racket as if she were surprised to find it in her hand. Waving it nonchalantly, she said, "I really can't stay. We'll make plans for some other time."

Reid looked surprised and disappointed as he came to her. "I suppose if you have other plans, I understand. I just thought . . ."

"How about Friday? Would you like to come over to my place for dinner?" Behind him, Megan saw the girls exchange an angry look.

"Sure. You live on Appletree, you said. What number?"

"It's 931, the peach-colored house with blue shutters. Say about eight?"

"Eight is fine. I'll see you then." When Reid smiled at her, Megan felt as if the day hadn't been a total loss.

As she turned to walk away, Megan heard Jeanette repeat, "If she wasn't going to play tennis, why was she carrying a tennis racket?"

"Don't be so dense," Terry hissed at her sister.

Megan walked faster. Reid and his daughters might dote on each other, but clearly there was no room for an extra person in their relationship. "It's a good thing he's decided not to remarry," she muttered wryly as she started her car. "Those girls would probably lynch a candidate for stepmother."

Reid dressed carefully Friday evening. All week he had thought of Megan and wondered if she was as special as she seemed. She was so vibrant, so alive, easy going yet crackling with energy. And she played it straight, with no coyness or simpering delicacy. Altogether a pleasing, entrancing woman. Terry and Jeanette hadn't acted too interested in her, but he knew how jealously they guarded their time with him. He should have prepared them for a foursome at tennis. Their coolness was his own fault for surprising them. After Megan left he had explained to them that the woman was a friend of his—only a friend. Soon the girls had seemed to put her out of their minds.

He shook his head. He'd never understand teenagers. One minute they were children, vying for his attention, and at the next they behaved like sensible adults. Reid found them lovable and fascinating, and he was sure Megan would, too.

He paused and looked at himself in the mirror. Hell. There was Megan, stealing his attention again. Why was he so preoccupied with this woman? She seemed to enter all his thoughts. He hoped he wasn't falling for her. Not after her declaration of wanting to remain emotionally unencumbered. Reid wasn't opposed to an affair, but he knew he was the sort of person who would want to marry if he fell in love. He suspected that that was hopelessly old-fashioned, but that was the way he was, so he was particularly careful not to fall in love in the first place.

Suddenly he realized what he was thinking, and he frowned. Marriage? Love? Who said anything about wanting to get married? Not he! He enjoyed weekends of not having to repair the plumbing or paint the den. No more marriage worries for him!

When he reached Megan's house he studied it carefully. Even without the house number, he would have known it was hers. The house was eclectic, just like its owner. Beds of yellow mums bordered the walk and circled the two trees. On the porch hung an old-fashioned courting swing. A blue wooden stencil spelling out the name Wayne hung on the door below an etched-glass window. Stained-glass hangings in the front bay windows glowed like jewels from the light within. Above the mailbox was a Pennsylvania Dutch hex sign of two birds surrounded by hearts and tulips. Reid knocked on the door as he studied the unusual design in the etched glass. He had never seen one quite like it, and he decided that that, too, suited the place Megan would live in.

Megan answered at once and greeted him with a smile. "Come in, Reid. You're in for a rare treat tonight."

"Oh?" As he drank in the visual feast of Megan herself, he sniffed the pleasant aromas of cooking but couldn't place any particular smell. "I like your dress."

Megan looked down and ran her hands over the simple lines of the green dress. The long sleeves fit closely, and the bodice was snug beneath her breasts before flowing into an empire skirt. "It's not quite right for the meal, but it's the closest thing I had on hand. You see, we're going on a journey tonight. To medieval England."

"What?"

"I'm writing an article for a gourmet magazine. My theme is medieval cooking. Here, let me take your coat." She hung it on a brass coatrack and led him through a white gingerbread arch into the living room and on to the kitchen.

"Did you say medieval food?"

"Yes. Do you like it?"

"I have no idea."

"Good! It'll be an adventure." She went to the stove and dipped them each a goblet of what looked like dark-red wine. "This is hippocras. Careful. I sometimes get it too hot."

Reid tasted the ruby liquid and smiled his approval. At the second swallow, an explosion of warmth bloomed in his stomach and flowed like heady lava throughout his body. "Interesting."

"It's quite strong," she said. "I like it, though."

The dining-room table was set, the room lit only by candles. After half a glass of hippocras, Reid saw nothing odd about drinking medieval wine in a room decorated with American Indian and African tribal masks.

As he helped Megan bring in the unusual foods, she told him their exotic names, but he promptly forgot them. He was much more interested in Megan. Instead of serving the dishes in courses, as one would have in the fifteenth century or earlier, she explained, they would put everything on the table at once to save steps.

"All this for two people? Or is the Queen of England dropping by later?" he teased.

"Most of these recipes can't be prepared successfully in smaller portions. Like the farced chicken, for instance. How can you stuff half a bird? I'll have to freeze the leftovers. At least you can see why I wanted company to help me eat it."

"So now we hear the real reason I was invited," he said with a grin.

She glanced at him over her shoulder and smiled. "That's not the reason." For a moment excitement thrummed between them, but then she was off to the kitchen again.

When the table was full, she viewed it with approval. "There now. Let's eat."

"You forgot the plates."

"No, I didn't. We're going to use these trenchers."

"They look like half loaves of Italian bread."

"They are. I didn't have time to bake the real thing."

Reid followed her example and gingerly ladled a dish called *hanoney* onto his trencher. "No forks?"

"They aren't invented yet. You have a knife and spoon."

He tasted the yellowish mixture and pronounced, "It's like scrambled eggs with crisp onions."

"That's exactly what it is. You expected hummingbird tongues, perhaps?" She passed him a plate of flat cakes. "This is tansy cake. I'm pretty sure you'll like it."

"Do you cook this way often?"

"No, but I've tried a few of these dishes before. I'd appreciate your honest reaction to each dish. My article, you know."

The farced chicken with its stuffing of cherries and oatmeal was a hit, as was the *chardwardon*—pears baked in a honey-cinnamon sauce. When Megan tasted the *le-*

monwhyt she wrinkled her nose in disapproval. So did Reid.

"I must have left something out. Wait a minute." She dashed into the kitchen and came back with the cookbook. "Rice," she read, "cinnamon, white wine, whole grated lemon."

"You grated the whole lemon? Rind and all?"

"That's what it says to do. Ha! Here it is. I forgot to garnish it with honey." She ran back into the kitchen and returned with a jar of honey.

She dribbled the sweet liquid liberally over the rice, then tasted it and met Reid's eyes as she again wrinkled her nose. "So much for *lemonwhyt*." She scribbled a note in the margin of her cookbook.

When the meal was over, Megan asked anxiously, "What did you think? Be honest."

"It was . . . very interesting."

"Would you eat it again?"

"Not if I had to include the *lemonwhyt*." His gleaming smile instantly took the sting out of his words.

Megan grinned, made some notes and put her notebook aside. "That was fun. Maybe I'll sell a couple of stories, using different angles, while the memory is still fresh." She began clearing the table. "Go into the living room and make yourself at home. I won't be but a minute."

"No way. I feel as strongly about being waited on as you do about having someone carry your picnic basket. I'll help you clean up."

"You mean you aren't one of those men who think every household duty has either 'male' or 'female' stamped on it?"

"Absolutely not."

She beamed. "I like that. I'm glad we decided to be friends." She turned briskly and hurried into the kitchen before he could see the expression she knew must be shining in her eyes. Most of the arguments she'd had with Hugh were over what was "woman's work" and what was not. They were arguments she had invariably lost.

Reid insisted on pushing up his sleeves and loading the dishwasher as she put the leftovers into freezer containers. She found herself staring at him as he worked. At the moment he didn't look at all like the successful demigod of the sporting-goods world. He looked like a husband.

She turned away abruptly. "That's it. I appreciate your help."

"That went fast with both of us working." He looked satisfied as he dried his hands and rolled down his sleeves.

Did he miss helping out in the kitchen? Megan wondered. Surely not. She was positive a person in Reid's position must have employed a maid. Megan had seen pictures of his ex-wife, whose name was now Pamela Bennett. There *had* to have been at least one maid. The woman looked too delicate to get a jar open by herself.

They went into the living room, and Megan added another log to the low fire. "I hope the meal wasn't too odd for you. I don't usually go overboard like that. With recipes, though, I have to taste them before I can describe them, and having another person's opinion is helpful. Did you mind?"

"Not at all."

"The idea came to me after I invited you. I suppose I should have warned you."

"You worry too much. I would have come anyway. I enjoyed it. I like trying new things."

She sat beside him on the rose-hued sofa. Picking up a small throw pillow, she said, "I'm afraid your daughters thought I was barging in last Saturday. That's why I left," she admitted.

"So that was it. I thought perhaps I had said something to upset you. You don't have to worry about them. They had had words with their mother over being able to come, and they were a bit on edge. They aren't really that hard to get to know."

Megan didn't believe him, but she held her tongue. "Will they be back tomorrow?"

"No. I usually only see them every other weekend and occasionally on a weeknight. Are you busy this weekend?"

"I don't have anything planned," she said carefully, not wanting to appear too eager.

"Would you like to do something with me?"

"Yes!" she blurted out, then blushed. "That would be nice," she said more demurely.

"You name it. We could drive down to Denver and go to the theater or maybe go dancing at one of the clubs."

"How about a walk in the woods, followed by a movie?"

"A movie?"

"That renovated theater is opening tonight, and tomorrow they're showing *Casablanca*. Do you like old movies?"

"I—I don't really know. I never gave it much thought."

"You mean you never watch the late shows? What do you do at night?"

"Frequently I have papers to look over, reports to read—things like that."

"That's terrible. I can see I'm going to have to make it my business to teach you how to play. Starting tomorrow."

He grinned. "I was under the impression you already *had* started. I don't know when I've enjoyed myself so much." Before she realized what he was doing, Reid leaned forward and kissed her.

At first his lips merely grazed hers, nudging them open as his fingers tilted her head back. Megan's eyes closed as she savored the sweetness of his breath and the longed-for sensation of a man's lips upon hers. Then she realized it was Reid's lips she hungered for, not just any man's. She met his kiss eagerly and sighed as he ran the tip of his tongue over her lips.

Reid pulled her closer and cradled her head in the crook of his arm as he kissed her more deeply. He ran his thumb over her cheek and jaw and threaded his strong fingers in her hair. Megan put her arms around him, feeling the roughness of his sweater and the hard muscles beneath. Her world whirled and dipped, and she forgot everything but the man in her arms.

Softly at first, then blazing brighter and brighter, something she dared not name flickered to life. An emotion she thought was gone forever filled her and sent its warmth throughout her mind and body.

When at last Reid pulled back, she could only stare at him. Her eyes were misty, and her dewy lips were still slightly parted. His expression was one of confusion, and a small muscle ridged in his jaw as he looked at her.

"Megan?" he asked softly, then stopped.

"Yes, Reid?" she whispered.

He looked even more confused and shook his head, not taking his eyes from hers. "I have to go," he murmured. Then more loudly he said, "Yes, I have to go. I wouldn't want to overstay my welcome." He looked as though he wanted to say more but wouldn't or couldn't. After a moment he said, "Yes, well, I'll see you tomorrow."

Megan nodded, not trusting herself to speak. The intensity of her attraction to Reid terrified her and at the same time seemed as inevitable as a spring rain. "Yes. Tomorrow," she finally said absently. She needed time to think. Time to convince herself she was wrong about her feelings for Reid Spencer. For too long she had equated love with agonizing loss. She wasn't ready to chance it again. Not now!

She watched Reid let himself out, and afterward she stared at the door. She couldn't possibly be falling in love with Reid Spencer, the one man who had stressed above all else that he wanted no permanent relationship! Numbly Megan sank back down onto the couch.

Chapter Three

When Reid arrived for their walk, Megan met him at the door with a wrench in her hand. "What's that for?" he asked.

"My kitchen sink is stopped up."

Reid sighed. This was far too reminiscent of his Saturdays with Pamela, and he wasn't in any mood to work on plumbing. Wearily he held out his hand. "Give me the wrench and show me what's wrong."

"Don't be silly," Megan said with a laugh. "I'm almost finished. You can keep me company."

"*You're* working on the plumbing?"

"Of course. It's not all that hard. I have a book on household repairs, and it's just a matter of following instructions," she said over her shoulder as she preceded him through the house.

Tools were scattered around the kitchen floor, and Reid could tell she had indeed been under the sink. The trap was off and had already been cleaned out. "Let me finish for you," he said gallantly.

"There's no point in both of us getting dirty." She showed him her smudged hands. "Sit there at the table and talk to me." As she spoke she sat on the floor and swung her upper torso under the sink.

Reid admired her jean-clad legs and how her sweat-shirt rode up to expose the wedge of pale skin at her waist. "You're the prettiest plumber I ever saw."

"Thanks," she replied with a laugh. "I had hoped to be through before you got here, but I had trouble getting the pipes loose."

"Why didn't you wait for me to do this for you?"

She swung around to look at him in surprise. "Why would I do that?"

"Usually men are the ones to do repairs. Especially a messy job like this."

"I never realized the ability to repair pipes was a sex-linked trait. Besides, it's my problem, not yours."

He sat on the floor beside her and handed her a washer when she groped for it.

"Hugh was sick for so long that I had to learn to do things for myself," she explained as she put the washer in place and threaded the nut back on. "His medical bills were so high that we couldn't afford outside services for every little thing that went wrong."

"I know it's none of my business, but is money still that tight? Is that why you're doing this yourself?"

"No, I'm making a comfortable living. The house is paid for, and I have no major bills now. I'm doing this because I see no reason to pay someone to do something I can do quicker and with less mess. Have you seen what some plumbers do to a room?" She fitted the wrench in place and tugged the nut tight. "Will you turn on the water for me?"

Reid stood and turned the faucet experimentally.

"Ha!" Megan chortled. "It's fixed."

Reid grinned down at her. "Lady, you're something else." He held out his hand and pulled her to her feet.

Megan shoved a stray lock of hair from her eyes. "As soon as I put away the tools and clean up, we can go. I hope you haven't minded the wait."

"I've enjoyed it."

She gave him a puzzled smile as she gathered the tools into her tool chest and shoved it into the pantry. As she mopped up the mess in front of the sink, she said, "I have a particular place in mind for our walk, if you don't already have anywhere special you want to go."

"Any place is fine with me."

"I got an idea for an article on folk crafts, and I know a group of artisans who live in the mountains. I thought we might go there as well."

"That's fine with me."

Megan stood the mop outside to dry and said, "Make yourself at home. I won't be long."

She hurried upstairs and glanced at her face in the bathroom mirror. "Damn," she muttered. In her rush to repair the sink she had forgotten to put on makeup, and after her struggle with the pipes, one cheek had a dark streak across it. "At least he won't think you're trying to dazzle him with sophistication," she told herself darkly. "Of all the days for the sink to stop up!"

She scrubbed herself clean and nearly ran into the bedroom as she stripped off her sweatshirt. She wanted to impress Reid, not put him off. Quickly she put on a clean pair of jeans and grabbed a sweater from a dresser drawer. The sweater was new, a pale green Irish knit with a stripe of darker green around the shoulders. She pulled it on and ran her fingers through her tousled hair. As fast as she could, she put on makeup and brushed her hair. If only Reid had been a little late, she would have looked quite nice. She studied her fingernails to be sure they were clean as she stepped into her Topsiders. As she hurried out the door, she fastened a small opal pendant around her neck.

"That was fast," Reid said in surprise when she came downstairs.

"I didn't want to keep you waiting." She went to the hall closet and took out a fleecy white melton jacket. "Are you ready to go?" They went outside, and she automatically headed for her car.

"We'll take mine this time."

"But it was my idea, and I don't know what the roads are like after the rain we had last week."

"Come on." He took her arm, led her to his car and opened the passenger door. "You're the most independent woman I've ever met."

"Do you mind?"

"Not in the least." He grinned. "In fact, I like it a lot."

Megan smiled as she slid into the car, but she wasn't convinced. "Hugh frequently complained about my wanting to do things for myself," she told him as he backed out of the drive. "He said I was macho."

Reid laughed and glanced over at her. "That's not exactly the way I'd describe you."

"Maybe it's because he hated becoming weaker and saw me becoming stronger to compensate."

"That's probably it."

"But I never minded. If I were the one who had gotten sick, he would have taken care of me."

Reid looked at her curiously. "Are you trying to convince me or yourself?"

"You, of course," she said as she looked away. "I don't want you to think I felt like a martyr, because I didn't."

"I see."

"Well, I didn't!" She frowned at the passing scenery. *Was* she trying to convince herself? "I loved him. When he died, I was devastated. At first I was angry over his leaving me—" She stopped abruptly. She had almost said, "After all I had done."

Reid reached out and took her hand. She let herself enjoy the feel of his warm skin on hers, the way his fingers covered hers with protective strength. But suddenly she felt an icy dread, and she pulled away.

"I'm sorry. I know you must have loved him a great deal. I didn't mean to overstep the bounds of propriety."

"You didn't." Megan felt ridiculous to have pulled away when she had been enjoying his closeness so much. Reid was no casual acquaintance in her mind, even though they had known each other such a short while. She liked him a great deal. Maybe more than that. Again the fear crept over her, and she frowned. What was going on here?

She looked over at him in the pretense of studying the approaching mountains. He was all any woman would dream of in a man: handsome, successful, companionable, incredibly sexy. His silver hair contrasted sensually with the strong lines of his face, and his body was magnificent. So why did she feel this fear whenever she thought of her emotions toward him?

"I wasn't that fortunate in my marriage," he was saying. "About the only good thing that came of it were my daughters.'' He grinned again. ''They say a daughter is special to her father, and it's true. I've always been closer to them than I was to Pamela.''

''You must have been happy in the beginning.''

''Maybe. If I was, I don't recall it. Pamela is weak, always needing to be taken care of and always wanting more than I could give.'' He smiled wryly, and his voice was dry as he said, ''I guess I'm just not cut out to be a husband.''

''I wouldn't say that,'' she said before she thought. Immediately a bright blush colored her cheeks. ''Here's the turnoff,'' she said to cover her embarrassment.

The road narrowed and climbed steeply up the side of the mountain. Oaks and sumacs gave way to the birches and maples of the higher elevation. At the word *husband*, Megan suddenly knew why she was so fearful of her feelings for Reid. She was afraid of being tied down again. Of losing her freedom.

Reid glanced over at her. She was awfully quiet all of a sudden. He supposed she was concentrating on finding their destination, and he took the opportunity to study her. Had he thought she was pretty? She was beautiful. He liked the way her thick hair fell in waves to her shoulders; he liked the stubborn line of her chin and jaw. Her eyes had the hues of the woodlands in them, as well as sharp intelligence. She was athletically slender without being willowy, and her hands and movements showed her confident capability. From the very start she had struck him as unusual and intriguing. He wanted more from her than friendship, yet he wasn't after a casual affair, either. Sex with no commitment or deep feelings didn't interest Reid. He frowned slightly as he tried to figure out exactly what he *did* want from her.

''Turn left,'' she instructed.

And another thing, he thought. She wasn't carrying a purse. He had never known Pamela to cross the threshold without her enormous assortment of makeup, credit cards, keys, brush and comb and whatever else she deemed necessary for survival away from the house. He'd bet Megan didn't taken an entire wardrobe on trips, either.

Megan was having a great deal of difficulty keeping her mind on remembering how to reach the home of her acquaintance. Reid seemed so close, and her nerves seemed attuned to his slightest movement. She wanted him to take her hand, but after the way she had pulled back before, she knew he wouldn't reach out again. Nor did she feel confident enough to reach out to him. She tried to keep from sighing in frustration. Why did he affect her like this? She had dated several men during her years as a widow, and none of them had been so disturbing.

Their destination, a handful of primitive log cabins, was at the end of a bumpy one-lane road. Several children were playing in the dirt, and they stopped to stare as two mongrels ran up to the car, barking a warning.

"Are you sure about this?" Reid asked doubtfully.

"It's all right. Come on."

Before he could stop her, Megan was out of the car and walking confidently toward the children. Reid was quick to join her.

A thin man came out of the nearest cabin and whistled at the dogs before turning his unwelcoming stare at the visitors. Then his face crinkled in a wide smile. "Megan! I didn't expect you today." He pushed his thinning hair back from his face as he called over his shoulder, "Feather, Luke. Megan is here!" He led them to the cabin.

"Feather?" Reid queried Megan in a low voice.

"I met these people when I was doing an article about what happened to the flower children of the late sixties," she whispered. To the lanky man, she said, "Micah, this is a friend of mine, Reid Spencer. Reid, this is Micah and his wife, Feather. Luke and Pleasant are over there by the loom."

A gaunt woman with unusually long hair and a happy smile came to hug Megan. "It's so good to see you again. Can you stay a few days?"

"Not this time, Feather. I'm doing another article, this time on handicrafts. May I interview you?"

"Of course." Feather's voice was soft and as calm as her contented features.

"You have a very unusual name," Reid said.

"Oh, it's not the one I was born with. My parents named me Barbara, but it was never me, you know? I think that choosing our own names is more sensible, don't you?"

"What about your children? You named them, didn't you?" he asked, with growing curiosity.

"Sure. You have to put something on a birth certificate or they can't go to school. When they're older they can change them if they want to. Incidentally, they're my grandchildren. Pleasant is my daughter. You'll see my sons out back. Come in. Come in. Don't stand here at the door."

When they stepped farther into the log cabin, Reid saw that it was a large workroom, rather than a house as he had assumed. Behind the large loom were baskets of dyed yarn and shelves of folded cloth. In the center of the room was a massive table, scarred from years of work. On it lay a dulcimer in the last stages of construction.

"You came at a good time," Micah said. "We're taking the latest bunch down to the trade center tomorrow."

"They sell their crafts and weaving to tourists through the trade center outside Estes Park," Megan explained.

"We don't need much." Pleasant spoke from the loom. "We're almost entirely self-sufficient."

"What about the children? Don't they go to school?"

"Of course. Luke drives them down to the bus stop and goes after them when it's time for them to come home."

"Isn't that rather inconvenient?"

"No. They're our children." Pleasant looked at him as if he might be rather simpleminded. To Megan she said, "Look at this hanging I finished yesterday. Do you like it?"

"It's beautiful!" Megan held the gaily colored cloth up so Reid could see it. The design, one of Pleasant's own creations, combined the colors of sunset with a shape resembling a mountain range. The woven undulations seemed to flow across the heavy fabric. "I think it's your best one."

"It's yours."

"I couldn't possibly take it," Megan protested.

"Please. I want you to."

Megan smiled as she ran her hand over the cloth. "Thank you, Pleasant. I'll always treasure it."

"Come out back and see the boys," Micah said. "They're busy and can't come inside."

They went out to the backyard, where Micah's adult sons were boiling large pots of dye.

"Benjamin, Joshua, this is Megan's friend, Reid. Megan's back to write another article."

The men smiled and nodded shyly but continued stirring the simmering mixtures. Megan stepped nearer, her notepad in hand. "What are you using for dye?"

"This yellow pot is marigolds," Feather said. "The pink is crab apples; the dark green is cockleburs. The purple comes from elderberries. We'll put the wool yarn in once the dye cools and is strained. You wouldn't want to use these dyes on linen or cotton. It won't work as well."

Micah nodded toward an enclosure where a number of sheep were penned. "We prefer to use wool, since we can grow our own. Now and then we have to buy a little cotton and linen, but silk is too expensive."

"We use alum as a mordant for all the colors but the cockleburs. By using an iron pot, we get the mordant for green automatically. If we added alum, it would turn a brownish color. Actually, a true green is very difficult to get."

Megan followed Feather and Micah around the yard and took copious notes on the dying process, how the yarn was prepared and how to beam the warp on the loom.

Reid found himself becoming fascinated with the unusual family and their eccentric way of life. Never had he met people like this, and it had never occurred to him to wonder how cloth was made.

Luke's talent was for wood carving, and Megan elicited anecdotes and made notes about the animals and birds he had fashioned after the wildlife he saw every day. He also had a number of walking sticks topped with quartz stones, which he sold through the various renaissance fairs that had recently become so popular all across the country.

Before they left, Micah took down some of his musical instruments and showed Reid how to play a dulcimer. "I send a few down to the trade center, but my best market for these is in the Blue Ridge. I ship them out to my cousin in Blowing Rock, North Carolina."

When Megan finished her notes she said reluctantly, "We really should be going. We've already taken up so much of your time. I can't thank you enough for letting me interview you."

"Any time," Micah said, and Feather nodded. They waved as Megan and Reid went back to his car.

Driving down the winding road, Reid mused, "I never heard their last name."

"I've never heard it either. They go only by the first names they've chosen."

"So that's where the flower children went."

"Only some of them. Most have jobs as normal as the rest of us."

"How did you ever meet these people in the first place?"

"I was in the trade center when they brought in a load of hangings and things. I started talking to Feather, and, as you can see, you can't talk to any of them without becoming friends. I don't think they have an enemy in the world."

"They certainly are unique."

"At times I envy them their peace and simple life."

Reid looked over at her. "I would have said your own life was pretty uncomplicated."

She laughed. "You've never seen me when a deadline is looming. I become absolutely frantic and bounce off the walls."

"Like when I wouldn't give you the interview?" he teased.

"You only saw the tip of the iceberg." She leaned forward. "Pull in here."

"Here? Why?"

"We're going for that walk in the woods I promised you."

Reid parked, and they strolled through a glade of aspens. Above them the vivid blue sky appeared in patches through the lacing of brilliant gold leaves shimmering in the breeze. Megan ran her hand over a white tree trunk. "Listen," she said. "You can hear the river."

They made their way down the slope to where a wide stream splashed over and around smooth rocks and emerald-mossed tree trunks. Megan climbed onto a boulder that jutted out over the water and sat down to dangle her feet over the edge.

Reid lowered himself beside her, and they gazed in contemplative silence at the rushing water.

"I've never seen this place before," he said.

"I used to come here often. It's one of my favorite thinking places. You wouldn't believe how many earth-shaking problems I've solved right here on this very rock."

Reid reached out and took her hand. Gently he placed her palm against his larger one, measuring her fingers to his, before enclosing her hand. After a moment he said, "Are you going to pull away again?"

"I don't think so," she said shakily.

"You don't know for sure?" His thumb was smoothing over her wrist and sending tiny flickers of fire up her arm.

"No. No, I'm not going to pull away."

Slowly, giving her ample warning, Reid leaned nearer. When only a breath separated their lips he asked, "Why did you pull back before?"

"You frighten me, in a way," she whispered, her breath almost stopping at his nearness.

"Am I frightening you now?"

"No." Her voice was barely audible, and when his lips closed over hers she went willingly into his embrace.

Reid knew all there was to know about kissing, she discovered. He knew exactly how to draw forth her response and to make her ache for more. The kiss deepened until Megan felt the world swirl beneath her, and she began to hope it would never end.

"You don't kiss like a woman who's frightened," he observed. "You kiss me as if you enjoy it a great deal."

"You confuse me," she said, drawing back. "I don't want to get involved right now. I just want us to be friends."

"Do you? Just platonic friends?" He lowered his head and left a trail of kisses along her neck and at the tender spot behind her ear. "I want more than that."

"What, Reid? What exactly do you want?"

He gazed deeply into her eyes before kissing her again in his sensuously expert way. His fingers laced through her hair, and he cupped her face with his palms as his lips seared hers.

"I don't want just to sleep with you," Megan forced herself to say. "As old-fashioned as it sounds, I'm really not that sort of a woman."

"I know you aren't." He was looking at her as if he were discovering a treasure.

"I'm not ready for anything more permanent, however," she tried to explain as she touched his face where the laugh lines creased his cheeks whenever he smiled. "I don't want to give up my freedom."

"I'm not asking you to. You can have a relationship and not lose any freedom at all."

"Can I? I don't see how that's possible."

"It can be done. Your friends up on the mountain there don't seem to lack freedom."

"That's different. They aren't me."

Reid reluctantly released her face and leaned his forearm on his bent knee. "Do you know what I think? I don't believe you're as worried about losing your freedom as you think you are. Oh, that's part of it, but I think you're more afraid of caring for someone and then losing him."

Megan drew in her breath sharply. Whether she wanted to admit it or not, his words struck home.

"Think about it, Megan. I'm not trying to take away your freedom. And I'm as healthy as the proverbial horse."

"What are you saying?" she whispered.

Reid looked away and stared at the water for a long time before answering. "I'm not sure. Probably too much." He paused again. "Okay, lady, I'll do as you want. We'll be friends."

"Platonic?"

"For as long as you want it that way." He looked back at her, and Megan felt herself becoming lost in his hypnotic gaze.

Slowly she nodded. He had brought something to life in her that she wasn't ready for, and she didn't want to admit it. She wondered if he knew just how accurate his words about her fears had been.

Falling in love with Reid Spencer or anyone else was not something she wanted. The very idea made her quake. If she let herself love Reid, she instinctively knew it would be deeper and more passionate than any love she had known before.

When Reid stood and held out his hand to help her to her feet, she was both relieved and frustrated that he had not insisted upon more.

Chapter Four

Megan dressed carefully for her date with Reid. Although he hadn't said so, she knew this evening was important to him. They were going to a cocktail party being given by one of Reid's closest friends, and most of his acquaintances would be there. Megan tried to tell herself this was no big deal and that she had never found it awkward to meet strangers—that it was, after all, only a date. But she knew Reid was taking her because he wanted his friends to meet her.

She slipped on a white dress of Victorian lace and buttoned the pearl fasteners on the tight sleeves. She had brushed her hair into a Gibson girl with soft tendrils that curled around her face and neck. The hairstyle complemented the romantic dress and lent her an aura of gentle sophistication. She wanted to make a good impression on his friends. Although she doubted Reid was overly sensitive about whether anyone approved of someone he was dating, she wasn't completely sure.

In her haste, Megan dropped the backing of one of her pearl earrings and frowned as she bent to retrieve it. Why should she assume that Reid didn't care what other people thought? she wondered. He had never told her that, and his actions hadn't particularly indicated that he felt that way. She was the one who normally didn't care whether others approved of her actions or the friends she chose.

She rested her chin on her palm and studied herself in her dresser mirror. If she did fail to impress his friends at the party, would Reid continue to date her? An icy chill swept through her when she couldn't immediately answer that question. Megan rose quickly to dispel her apprehension and padded across the soft carpet to get her heels from the top of her closet. If she had any reason to think this would be true, she shouldn't be going out with him at all.

Reid Spencer was becoming much too important to her. She had no desire to fall in love, just as she had no intention of remarrying. Her life was enjoyable and full of freedom. Being tied down again was no enticement to her. Then a tiny thought deep inside her whispered: not only that, but if you fall in love, you might lose him.

Megan looked back at the mirror as if she dreaded what she might find there. Was that really the major source of her reluctance? As she was shaking her head, the doorbell sounded. Quickly she grabbed her cashmere wool cape and headed downstairs, resolving that she would keep her emotions in check. A friendship with Reid was all she wanted.

Reid was dressed in a gray two-piece suit with a pale-blue shirt and a crimson tie. His eyes glowed a deep azure. Megan found herself staring at him. What had happened to her? All he had said was hello, and her defenses melted like warm butter. "You look very handsome tonight," she said to cover her confusion.

"I was just thinking how beautiful you are." His voice seemed to touch her soul, and his eyes were filled with an emotion Megan dared not examine too closely.

"Thank you." As he helped her with her cape, his fingers grazed her neck. Megan felt the sensation down to her toes.

As they drove to his friend's house, Reid carried the conversation. Megan was too shaken by the emotion dawning in her. She wasn't falling in love! She wouldn't! This was merely a chemical thing, a biological urge, she assured herself. Unfortunately, she knew better even as she thought it. Over the past three years she had had no sexual needs that affected her like this.

"You're awfully quiet tonight," he said.

"Am I?" she replied a bit too quickly. "I hadn't noticed."

"Are you nervous about meeting these people?"

"Of course not." Then she added, "Should I be?"

"Not in the least. Chad Merrick is my friend, as are most of the others, but that's certainly no reason to be nervous."

"I'm not nervous." She clutched her beaded bag as if to keep it from flying away.

"So I see. You'll have a good time, you know. If you don't, we'll leave."

She nodded. Shyness had seldom been a problem with her since she had become an adult, but she recognized the symptoms from her adolescence.

"Sometimes Chad's wife, Alice, gets carried away with her invitations, so there might be people there that I hardly know either. They don't necessarily agree on their choices of friends, and many of Alice's are stuffy bores. But don't worry—we'll avoid them.''

''They don't have the same friends?''

''Alice is forever trying to 'make something of Chad,' as she puts it. Actually, he's a very successful lawyer and was when they married. But she seems to think that constant contact with her elite social circle will somehow 'improve' him. I've always been rather surprised they've stayed together. They have very little in common.''

Just like us, Megan thought to herself. Reid was a go-getter—tough, determined, solid and the epitome of suave sophistication—whereas she was more the free-wheeling side, most comfortable in jeans and a sweat-shirt. It was far easier to imagine Reid with a dry martini than a can of beer, while she'd choose Budweiser over Tanqueray any day.

The Merricks' house was in an exclusive neighbor-hood that looked as if gardeners and landscape archi-tects must be part of each household's private staff. Expensive cars lined both sides of the street.

''It looks as if Alice invited everyone she knows,'' Reid commented as he parked. ''We may both choose to make this a short evening.''

Megan wondered at his words, but he was out of the car before she could question him. She was glad now that she had worn her most attractive dress; she had a feeling she was going to need all the confidence she could mus-ter.

They were ushered in by a uniformed maid, and Me-gan found herself in a sea of strangers. Reid put his arm around her and guided her to a man beside the table of hors d'oeuvres. When the man smiled at Reid, she relaxed. Surely any friend of Reid's would be friendly toward her.

"Megan, I want you to meet Chad Merrick. Chad, this is Megan Wayne."

"So you're Megan. I've heard a lot about you." Chad was almost as tall as Reid but lacked his distinctive features. He had a more homespun quality about him, which Megan found immediately endearing.

She gave him her hand and a smile. "I'm glad to meet you. You have a beautiful home."

Chad glanced around the elegant room. "I'm afraid I can't take any of the credit for it. My wife and her decorator rework it fairly often. That's the reason for the party. We're celebrating another face-lift for the house. Alice, come here and meet Reid's friend." A tall, cool blonde came to them, and Chad introduced her as his wife.

"I was just telling Chad what a lovely home you have," Megan said with sincerity and an open smile. "It's beautiful."

"Thank you." Alice was looking at her as if she wasn't quite sure Megan warranted her approval. "You have an unusual name. Is it short for Margaret?"

"No. It's just Megan."

Alice put out her arm to draw two other women into their circle. "Marcia, Catherine, this is Megan Wayne, Reid's new friend."

The two women greeted her with aloof politeness, and when Megan glanced at Reid, she found him frowning.

"If you'll excuse us, I want Megan to meet some of the others," he said abruptly.

"What was all that about?" Megan whispered as he whisked her away.

"When I asked you to come, I hadn't realized Alice was inviting this crowd."

"Who are they, and why were they so distant to me?"

"Catherine and Marcia are my ex-wife's closest friends. They take a dim view of seeing me here with anyone other than Pamela."

"But you've been divorced for two years!"

"I know, but they don't accept it any more than Pamela does." He drew her into another circle and introduced her to more of his friends.

Megan tried to connect the names and faces, but she was too distracted. Those two women and Alice had acted as if she were a pariah. She felt as though their eyes were boring into her back, and a glance over her shoulder confirmed it. By their expressions and the way they were leaning forward to speak to one another in undertones, Megan assumed she was the topic of their conversation. Chad cast his wife a disgusted look and came to join Megan.

Away from Alice, Megan discovered she liked Chad a lot. Soon they were laughing as if they were old friends, and she found herself enjoying the party. Maids and waiters glided silently through the crowd, offering hors d'oeuvres and martinis while unobtrusively removing empty glasses. Megan had seen parties like this in movies, but she had never attended one.

Chad was talented at telling jokes and reciting humorous anecdotes, and Megan was pleased to discover they shared the same sense of humor. They were soon swapping stories as if they had known each other for years. Chad put her completely at ease, and she felt good that she could just be herself. Reid was enjoying himself, too, and looked at Megan with obvious pride. There had been nothing for her to worry about after all.

From the corner of her eye, Megan saw Alice and Pamela's two best friends edging closer to them. She turned away. Nothing would be gained by letting them upset her. In a way it was admirable that they were so loyal to Pamela, even if the loyalty was over a dead issue. Chad recaptured Megan's attention by asking about her work, and she started telling him about some of the more interesting articles she had researched and written. She saw Reid's expression darken when he glanced at the three women, but Megan was too busy with her story to wonder why.

The conversation shifted, and Chad asked one of the other men a question about a local golf tournament. Megan wasn't particularly interested in golf, so she let her mind wander briefly.

Suddenly whisperings of "poor Pamela" and "not right for him" seemed to echo in her ears. She felt Reid stiffen beside her, and she listened to the words that were obviously meant for her to hear.

"When I think of all Pamela has gone through..." Marcia began.

"...I cringe," Catherine finished. "Thank goodness she wasn't able to come tonight. Can you imagine how she would have felt?"

"I was embarrassed for her," Alice put in. "When Reid said he was bringing someone, I naturally thought it would be one of our crowd. Not this *stranger*."

"Poor Pamela," Marcia repeated. "At least she was spared this."

"She simply doesn't fit in with our people at all, does she?" Alice said.

Megan's eyes flashed with anger, and she blushed to realize that conversation in her immediate circle had dwindled as everyone became aware of the women's words. Chad looked aghast, and Reid was clearly furious. Not one of them? Megan seethed. Embarrassed for Pamela? What kind of lowlife did they think she was?

Just then a waiter appeared with a tray of fresh martinis. Her anger about to boil over, Megan scooped the tray from his hand and balanced it over her shoulder. Emboldened by the astonished gasps erupting around her and armed with a brassy smile, she began serving the drinks with all the skills she had learned as a waitress in college. When the tray was empty, she handed it with a flourish to a stunned-looking Alice and turned to Reid. "Are you ready to leave?"

He was grinning his approval, his broad shoulders shaking with laughter. As they passed Chad, he lifted his glass to them in salute. From his expression Megan suspected he wished he could join them.

"You handled that beautifully!" Reid commented, still chuckling, when they were in the car.

"I stole the idea from the movie *Houseboat*. Sophia Loren did the same thing when she was in a similar situation."

"I still admire your spunk. That whole thing could have been a very awkward situation."

"What do you mean 'could have been'?" she asked wryly.

"It wasn't as awkward as it would have been if I'd said what I was about to say. You surprised the words right out of me."

"That's just as well. Being rude to them wouldn't have solved anything."

"It would have made me feel better." He reached out and took her hand. "You feel cold."

"I'm all right; I'm just upset. Reid, are you dating Pamela again?"

"Absolutely not."

"Have you considered going back to her? Those women seemed to think . . ."

"I don't care what they think. It was a bad marriage that got steadily worse. I have never once considered a reconciliation."

"Not even for your daughters' sake?"

"Living in a war zone wasn't good for them. Even if there hadn't been loud arguments—and there were a few of them—kids know when their parents don't get along. Nothing has changed. Remarriage would be worse for them than our divorce was. Besides, Terry is a senior, and Jeanette will graduate in two years. They'd soon be out of the house off to college, and I'd be stuck. No, I haven't even considering remarrying her. Get that idea out of your head."

Megan nodded. He sounded pretty positive on the subject. "I just wondered. I didn't want to stand in your way if you were considering it."

"I don't know why Alice and her friends chose to embarrass you like that. I'll see it never happens again."

"You don't have to rescue me. I wouldn't want you to do anything to spoil your friendship with Chad."

Reid smiled at her through the darkness. "You need rescuing less than anyone I've ever met."

"I'm beginning to feel a little bad about my behavior. Did I embarrass you?"

"On the contrary, I enjoyed it. You should have seen the look on those women's faces! No, I wasn't embarrassed."

"I'll bet Chad was. I shouldn't have done it."

"If anyone embarrassed Chad, which I'm not sure is possible, it was Alice, not you. Why are you doing this to yourself?"

"I tend to be too independent, and I sometimes go off on harebrained tangents. It's one of my worst faults."

"I like your independence, and you're not harebrained by anyone's definition."

"Hugh would have been mortified!"

Reid was silent for a moment, his tension suddenly mounting. "Hugh wasn't there. I was."

"I'm sorry. I didn't mean for it to sound like that." Megan looked at him in misery. "Please don't be hurt."

"Hurt? Not me." As the lights from an approaching car illuminated his face, Megan could see that he was clenching his jaw as if he were biting back words. "Try jealous."

"Jealous? Of Hugh?" Megan stared at him in surprise as he turned into her drive. "You're jealous over me?"

"You don't have to sound all that amazed. I shouldn't have said anything about it. Just forget it."

Megan's lips curved up in a smile. "I don't want to forget it. I don't think I've ever aroused jealousy in anyone in my entire life."

"Then you must have been married to a blind man. You're the most desirable woman I've ever met."

Megan looked away. "Don't. You mustn't say that."

Reid growled and silently cursed himself. How could he have been so insensitive as to find fault with her dead husband? On the other hand, did she think that Hugh had had no faults at all? That made him even more jealous. What kind of a paragon was he competing with?

Megan dared not trust herself to speak. She couldn't handle the idea that Reid found her so desirable. Not when she had struggled for days to view him platonically. She stole a glance and found him watching her.

Their eyes held for a timeless instant. "Would you like to come in? I can make some coffee."

"No, I don't think I'd better." He knew if he went into her house tonight that he would not want to leave before morning. He reached out and touched one of the curling tendrils on her neck. Would she mind if he told her how he was beginning to feel about her? Reid wasn't at all sure that he dared to voice those feelings, even to himself. If he did, wouldn't that mean a commitment, and wasn't he through with commitments forever? Of course he was, and with good reason! "I'd better be going."

She looked rather surprised but said, "I guess it is late. Maybe next time."

"Right." He started to get out to walk her to the door, but she stopped him.

"That's not necessary. I can let myself in." Once more she gazed into his eyes and felt overwhelmed by his nearness. "I've been coming and going by myself for years."

He put his hand behind her neck and tilted her face for his kiss as he pulled her closer. His lips were soft but firm on hers, and as the pressure of his mouth increased and his tongue met hers, she felt herself leaning closer so that the tips of her breasts brushed his chest. Sparks seemed to ignite throughout her and start a conflagration at her very center. Megan's soft moan bespoke her desire to let him sweep her away. It would be so easy to love him and let him love her. But suddenly, with her last ounce of reserve, she pulled away from the embrace. Quickly she got out of the car and hurried into the house without looking back.

Once she was safely inside, she leaned back against the door and closed her eyes. She should never have kissed him! She wanted him so badly that she ached. At the same time she was terrified of loving him and losing him, her independence, or both. But how could she stop something that seemed to be rushing through her life like a runaway train? With another low moan she pushed away from the door. Finally, she heard him start his car and drive away.

Megan had always preferred oil lamps to conventional lighting and often lit her hurricane lamps as dusk gathered. The days were growing short as autumn deepened, and she liked the cozy glow that softened the shadows in her living room.

She hadn't heard from Reid since the party two nights before, and she had debated about calling him all day. When the phone rang she jumped, almost dropping the glass chimney of the lamp she was lighting. She hurried to the phone and answered breathlessly.

When she heard a woman's voice on the other end, Megan felt instant disappointment but deftly covered it. "Who did you say this is? Susan! I haven't heard from you in ages."

"I'm no longer with *Trail Guide* magazine," the woman said. "I have a new job now. Guess where."

"I have no idea." Megan sat in the nearest chair, her legs curled over the arm. Susan Parsons had been her editor at *Trail Guide* for years, and during that time they had become friends, though they were both so busy they seldom wrote or talked unless it was related to business.

"*National Geographic*! How's that for coming up in the world?"

"That's wonderful!"

"Not only that, I have a story I want written, and you're just the person I want to write it."

"Me? For *National Geographic*?"

"Don't sound so surprised. You're good. Your research is impeccable. That's why I want you for this story."

"Tell me about it! What's the subject?"

"One I know you're interested in. The vanishing savannas in Africa and the threat civilization is posing to the wildlife."

"Africa?" A tiny shadow of apprehension crept over her.

"You'd write on location, of course. We can fly you over in a week or two. With luck you'll miss most of the winter here. I know what a problem snow is in Colorado. Think of it—you'll be basking in the sun and writing a story that will gain you worldwide recognition while all your friends are fighting snow and traffic snarls."

"All winter? In Africa?" Megan said bleakly.

"I thought you'd sound more pleased. I expected you to jump at the opportunity. With Hugh gone, it's not as if you can't get away."

"No, no, of course not. This is just such a surprise." Megan managed to keep her voice light, even as a rock seemed to be forming in her middle. "Are you sure it will take so long?"

"I'm positive. We like to be very thorough, you know. That's what makes us the best." Susan laughed and said, "I guess this was a bigger surprise than I thought it would be. Think it over and call me back. Just don't wait too long."

"Yes. Yes, I need to think about this. When did you say I would leave?"

"Not before the end of next week, or maybe the one after. We're still trying to line up the photographers."

"All right, Susan. I'll get back to you as soon as I can. What's your new number?" Megan wrote down the number as a dozen thoughts flew through her mind. After she said goodbye and hung up, she continued to rest her hand on the phone. Africa. For the entire winter. *National Geographic*! News that would have left her breathless with joy a month before now merely left her stunned. The truth was, she didn't want to go. Not even for *National Geographic*.

When the phone in her lap rang, Megan jumped. "Hello?"

"Guess what I was just able to get," Reid said enthusiastically.

"I don't know. What?"

"Tickets for the play *The Rainbow Menagerie*. It's been sold out for a month. The only catch is, they're for tonight. Do you want to go?"

"Sure. What time?"

"Seven-thirty."

"I can be ready," Megan said.

"You don't sound too thrilled," Reid said. "Are you too tired to go?"

"Of course I'm excited, Reid. I'll see you in about an hour." She hung up and replaced the phone on the end table. She knew she should stay home and think about this dilemma with *National Geographic*, but she wanted to be with Reid. Numbly she went upstairs to dress.

When Reid arrived he said, "What's wrong with the lights? Did your electricity go off?"

"What? No, no. I like lamps." She bent and blew them out, one by one. She turned on an electric lamp and felt in her pocket to be certain she had her keys. "I'm ready."

"I still can't believe I got these tickets," Reid said as they drove to the playhouse. "This is supposed to be the play of the season. Everyone's been talking about it."

"What's it about?"

"I don't know. It's one of those touring companies rather than the local theater group. I heard it was immensely successful on Broadway."

They arrived at the theater and joined the crowd. Inside an usher took them to their seats. Megan waited expectantly. "I've never seen a Broadway play," she said. "Have you?"

"A few times."

The lights dimmed, and a hush stole over the audience. The curtain made a whooshing sound as it swept back to reveal an almost empty stage with two straight chairs, a fake window hung from wires and a doorway set in the back curtains. Two actors in jeans and sweatshirts entered and engaged in a confusing conversation accompanied by exaggerated gestures.

Megan's mind wandered back to her conversation with Susan. Why was she so reluctant to take the step that could be the turning point of her career? Susan hadn't said so, but Megan knew this was tantamount to being offered a position on the staff of the prestigious magazine. She had thought *National Geographic* didn't use free-lance writers. That must mean a permanent move and lots of travel, exactly the sort of job she would have given anything to get before she had met Reid.

Guiltily Megan realized she wasn't paying any attention to the play, and she tried to focus on the frenzied actors. Their dialogue was silly as well as mildly irritating, and the entire plot, if there was one, seemed to hinge on innuendos and some nebulous problem with someone named Eleanora. Megan's mind wandered again.

She knew why she wasn't jumping at the offer. She wanted to stay near Reid. Megan felt disgusted with herself. He had shown no indication that he wanted her on a permanent basis, and she knew she would be foolish to risk her career on the chance that he might want her someday. Mentally she shook herself. She herself didn't want a commitment! She would call Susan back first thing in the morning and tell her she was already packing.

But then Reid reached over and took her hand, and Megan's confusion returned. Was her career really more important than Reid?

With great determination she forced her attention back to the actors. One man was flouncing around the stage in a catty imitation of Eleanora while the other chastised him. Megan smothered a yawn. Perhaps she had missed some crucial element, but the play was incredibly boring.

"How do you like it?" Reid whispered as the curtain closed on the second act.

"Terrific," she said as she tried to hide another yawn.

He grinned. "I think it's as boring as hell."

"So do I. Let's leave."

"As quickly as possible."

They left the theater and walked back toward Reid's car. Megan put her hand in his and matched her steps to his pace. "Look," she said as they neared the movie theater. "*Dracula* is playing." As they neared, she said, "It's the old Bela Lugosi one! Let's go in."

"To a vampire movie?"

"Sure. Halloween is right around the corner. This will put you in the mood."

"A vampire movie?" he repeated. "I haven't seen one since I was a kid."

"Then it's time you did. Come on. It's my treat." She overcame his objections and paid for their tickets.

They bought sodas and an enormous bag of popcorn and felt their way into the dark theater. Even as their eyes adjusted to the dimness the movie came on, and they wriggled down in their seats, the popcorn nestled between them.

Afterward they laughed and jostled each other on the way back to Reid's car. "There!" Megan said triumphantly. "Didn't I say you'd enjoy it?"

"I did for a fact, a lot more than that ridiculous play. How do you suppose that ever got on Broadway?"

"Maybe it was Broadway in Moose Jaw, Maine, instead of the one in New York."

"I never thought of that."

"Anyway, nothing beats old movies. I'm a real addict. When I was growing up I used to stay up half the night to see the late shows. I still do."

"I had forgotten how much fun they can be." They got into his car, and he drove through the quiet streets toward Megan's house.

"I'm sorry the play didn't turn out as well as you expected."

"Can't win them all." He had been thinking about that play and wondering why he had wanted to go. He didn't like the answer. He had bought the tickets because it was the sort of thing Pamela would have loved—avant-garde and abstract to the nth degree. He didn't like that sort of entertainment, and neither did Megan.

He glanced over at her. "The girls are coming over tomorrow. Would you like to have dinner with us?"

"Would they feel I'd be intruding?"

"Of course not. Why would they?"

"I just wondered. I know their time with you is limited."

"I want them to get to know you. It's important to me." He was beginning to care a great deal for Megan, and he wanted to share his daughters with her. Once she knew them, she'd really enjoy them. He tried to tell himself it was nothing more than that.

"All right. I'd like to have dinner with you. Should I bring anything?"

"Just yourself. Do you want me to pick you up at about seven?"

"No, I'll walk over."

Reid smiled. He liked Megan a great deal indeed.

Chapter Five

Reid, I've been thinking," Megan said as she cradled the phone against her shoulder. "Why not let me cook the meal. Then you'll have more time to spend with your daughters."

"I can't impose on you like that."

"Nonsense. I want to do it. I can find my way around your kitchen if you show me where you keep things."

"Well, I have to admit that I'm not much of a cook. That steak we had proves it."

"Then it's settled. I'll be there at six. What would you like to eat?"

"I'll buy the food. I was planning to stop at the grocery store on my way to pick up the girls."

"No, no. I'll bring it. The fact is, I'm not a terrific cook either, but I have some recipes I shine on. Let me impress you."

"You talked me into it. I'll see you later."

Megan smiled as she hung up. While she was no gourmet, she had some recipes that always earned her compliments. She had learned to cook in Charlotte, and her southern dishes were unrivaled.

Promptly at six, Megan arrived at Reid's house. Her palms were sweaty, and she had butterflies in her stomach over the prospect of meeting his daughters again. All afternoon she had told herself that they had merely been in a bad mood the day she met them. This time they would be expecting her, and she would see them as the darlings Reid described.

Juggling two sacks of groceries, Megan managed to ring the bell. On the second ring, Reid swung open the door.

"Come in, come in. Here, let me take that. I guess the girls didn't hear the doorbell. Jeanette, Terry, Megan is here."

She looked around expectantly, but neither girl appeared.

"They must be engrossed in the television. Come into the den."

She followed him through the living room and into the small den off the kitchen. Both girls were there, draped over chairs, listening intently to a rock video.

"Megan's here," Reid repeated.

"Hi," said Jeanette.

"Hi," said Terry. Neither evinced any enthusiasm.

"Who's that? Madonna?" Megan asked. "She's very good."

Terry gave her a level look and turned up the volume slightly.

Megan hesitated. She could hear Reid bustling around in the kitchen and knew she was alone with the girls. "I always liked the Beatles when I was your age."

"They're old-fashioned," Jeanette said disparagingly.

"They weren't at the time. In fact, they were considered quite risqué, with their long hair and all."

"Long?" Terry asked with contempt.

Megan looked at a close-up shot of the drummer, whose hair was roughly twice as long as her own. "It seemed long at the time."

Reid came back into the den and put his arm around Megan's shoulders. "How about if I help you cook?"

"Maybe the girls would like to," she said in sudden inspiration. She and her mother had always shared a special intimacy in the kitchen. "Terry, Jeanette? Will you give me a hand?"

The girls exchanged a look, and Terry sighed as if she were being asked to martyr herself. "Sure. Why not?"

Megan pointed Reid toward an easy chair. "You read the paper. We'll call you when it's ready."

"Want your pipe and slippers?" Terry asked sarcastically.

"You know I don't smoke," he said with a laugh. "Get out of here."

Jeanette smiled, and Megan was reminded of Reid. They had the same mouth and eyes. She put out her hand to touch Jeanette's arm as Reid bent to pick up the paper. Jeanette pulled away.

Megan shrugged. Some people didn't like to be touched. She went into the kitchen and started taking things out of the two bags. "This is a casserole I especially like," she said as she worked. From the den she heard strains of an easy-listening radio station replacing the rock music. "Terry, will you turn on the oven?"

Terry turned the dial and hoisted herself onto the countertop as Jeanette dropped into a chair at the breakfast table.

"I need a skillet, Reid," Megan called out.

"It's in there," Jeanette said, pointing at a cabinet to the right of the dishwasher.

"Of course. You'd know where to find everything, wouldn't you?" Megan said brightly.

"We're over here a lot. He's our father, you know."

"Yes, I know. Terry, where's the salt?"

"Dad?" she yelled from her perch on the counter. "Where's the salt?"

"In the pantry, where it always is," Reid called back. "Do you need any help?"

"No, everything's under control," Megan answered. She went to the pantry and got the box of salt.

She crumbled a package of ground beef into the skillet to brown. "Terry, will you watch this for me? Jeanette, I'd like for you to set the table, please."

Again the girls exchanged a rebellious look, but they obeyed. Megan tried to keep her hands steady as she measured the ingredients for corn bread. Then she opened the refrigerator and searched through its contents. "I can't find any bacon drippings," she said, bemused.

"Bacon what? Dad doesn't keep stuff like that," Terry said in disgust.

"No bacon drippings?" Megan had thought everyone saved some for cooking.

"That's not only disgusting, it's the worst type of cholesterol! What are you making, anyway?"

"It's a casserole of ground beef and pinto beans with a top layer of corn bread." Megan took out a bottle of vegetable oil and wondered if that would do as a substitute.

"It sounds awful."

"Actually, it's very good. You'll see."

"I wouldn't bet on it. Here. You stir the meat. I'm going to make a salad."

"I had planned to have—"

"Dad likes salad, and he likes it the way I make it," Terry interrupted, glaring at Megan as if she dared her to object.

"Suit yourself." Megan turned back to her corn bread and decided the oil would be better than nothing at all. Terry was rummaging through the refrigerator.

"What kind of dressing is there?" Megan asked as she opened a can of tomato paste. "I didn't bring any."

"Bottled dressing? We never eat that stuff. Mom and I make our own."

"Oh?" Megan stirred the drained meat into the casserole dish along with the beans and tomato sauce. The corn-bread batter didn't have quite the same consistency as it did when she made it at home.

"Mom says a real cook does everything from scratch. Jeanette, make those cute napkin folds the way Mom showed you."

Megan poured the corn-bread batter over the beans and looked over her shoulder to see Jeanette deftly folding the napkins into the shape of doves. "That's very pretty, Jeanette."

"You don't have to sound so surprised. I'm not a little kid."

"I never thought you were." Megan put the casserole into the oven and straightened. "Did it take long to learn how to do that?"

"Not too long. Mom has lots of patience. She showed me how. She says a meal should look good as well as taste good."

Terry took a paring knife and began to make radish roses for the salad. "Remember the time we had that taffy pull?"

Jeanette laughed. "Mom had a new recipe, and we all had to try it. Taffy takes couples, you know. She and Dad kept getting tangled up."

"You goose. They did that on purpose," Terry explained.

"We laughed until my sides ached."

Megan's own smile wavered. She had known, of course, that there had been good times in Reid's marriage, but hearing about one of them made her surprisingly jealous.

"And the time we went skiing and Mom fell," Terry added with a sidelong glance at Megan. "Dad scooped her into his arms and carried her all the way back to the lodge and up to their room."

"Dad's strong."

"Mom doesn't weigh much either. She's only a size seven."

Megan thought of the pounds she had been meaning to shed and made no comment.

"And the time Dad bought Mom that puppy and it cried so much he had to let it sleep with them?"

"Did you finish setting the table?" Megan asked in a tight voice.

"Sure. I used the good china. Mom says dinner should be eaten in style, not gulped down like lunch."

Megan, who frequently ate off paper plates to avoid washing dishes, nodded silently. Pamela was beginning to sound like a hearth goddess. Maybe Reid was wrong about not considering remarriage. The woman sounded perfect. She took out the balls of refrigerated pie crust she had taken from her freezer at home and looked for a rolling pin.

"What's that stuff?" Terry asked.

"It's going to be a cherry cobbler. Doesn't that sound good?"

"We never eat things like that. It's not good for you."

"Makes you fat," Jeanette added. "Dad hates dessert."

Megan faltered, but she was too far along to gracefully stop now. "He's never tasted my cobbler," she said with false confidence.

The casserole seemed to take forever to cook, and by the time it was brown on top, Megan was heartily sick of hearing about Pamela and how happy they had all been as a family.

"Reid, come and eat," Megan called as she and the girls carried the food to the table.

"Smells terrific. What is that?"

"That's what I asked," Terry said in an undertone.

"It's a casserole." Megan sat down in the nearest chair.

"That's my place," Jeanette objected. "I always sit beside Dad."

"This time you sit opposite me. That salad is a work of art, Megan."

"I made it," Terry said.

"And these napkins. You went to a lot of trouble."

Jeanette spoke up. "I did the napkins."

"They were a tremendous help," Megan put in. She noticed that Jeanette had even lit candles. The corn-bread casserole looked ridiculous served on delicate china amid crystal stemware.

Reid put a hefty serving of casserole onto his plate and said, "Hey, there's something under the corn bread after all!"

Megan knew he was teasing her, but she had to force a smile; she was in no mood for jokes. "Would you like me to serve you, Jeanette? The bowl is too hot to pass."

"Just a little."

"None for me," Terry said, "I'm a vegetarian."

"You are?" Megan felt her spirits droop.

"Since when?" Reid asked as he helped himself to the salad.

"I'm on a health program. I'm trying to cleanse my body of impurities."

"I see." He gave Megan an amused glance. "Like the time you took up yoga?"

"I still do yoga when I have time." Terry lifted her chin proudly. "I'm going to be a great actress someday, and I must experience everything."

"Experience passing me the corn," Reid suggested. "This meal is really good."

Megan took a bite of casserole and paused before chewing. The corn bread tasted greasy from the vegetable oil, and the whole dish was too salty. "Did either of you add salt to this?"

"No," Terry said innocently.

"Is it supposed to taste like this?" Jeanette asked as she poked at it with her fork.

Thoughtfully Megan regarded Terry. "No, it isn't."

"Must be the strange kitchen," Reid said. "I've heard women say they can't cook in anyone else's house."

"What women, Dad?"

"I've heard Mom say that," Terry answered.

Megan forced her attention to the food. She had wanted so badly for everything to work out.

"It's really not bad," Jeanette said. When Terry glared at her she added, "Once you get used to it."

"I like it. I don't think it's so salty," Reid said.

"Next time I'll make it at my house, and you can see how it's supposed to taste."

"Dad, remember the time Mom burned my birthday dinner, and we all went to that cute little Italian restaurant?"

"You remember that, Jeanette? You were only six."

"And the vacation where we went to the beach and you sent Jeanette and me out to look for seashells at dawn?"

"Eat your dinner," he ordered brusquely.

"Excuse me," Megan said as she stood up. "I have to check on the dessert."

In the privacy of the kitchen Megan gripped the edge of the countertop and forced herself to breathe normally. The girls were bound to have many pleasant memories. Now that Reid no longer lived with them, they must bring those memories out to prove to themselves that they had once been a family unit. Logically Megan knew that; emotionally she felt as if a knife were twisting in her middle. She heard Reid laugh in the next room, and she closed her eyes against the pain. What memory of his wonderful life with Pamela were the girls presenting him with now?

"Megan? Do you need help?" he called out.

"No, I can manage." She took the steaming cobbler out of the oven and carried it to the table.

"Cobbler. You're kidding!" he exclaimed.

"I told her we don't eat dessert," Terry said sanctimoniously.

"Speak for yourself. I love cobbler," Reid said. "I haven't had a good one in years."

Megan sat down with a smile of relief. Her cobblers never failed.

After dinner, Reid sat back and smiled. "That was great! Between the three of you, you work wonders."

"I'm glad you liked it." Megan began to clear the table.

"Let the girls do that."

She saw Terry's sullen expression and said, "It's no trouble. I want to do it."

"Then I'll help you."

"You're going to wash dishes?" Terry exclaimed.

"You never had to help Mom."

"Your mother has a maid."

Megan carried the dishes into the kitchen as Reid rolled up his sleeves. She could have cheerfully wrung both girls' necks.

"It's going well, isn't it?" Reid said as he loaded the dishwasher. "I could hear the three of you talking nonstop in here as I read the paper."

"Could you hear what we said?"

"Not with the music playing, but it sounded sweeter to me than the songs on the stereo."

Megan made no comment.

"I'm glad to see you're getting along so well with the girls. They've missed having a homey environment over here as well as at home. The divorce happened when they were at particularly vulnerable ages."

Megan saw no shred of vulnerability in either girl, so she pretended to be engrossed in sponging off the stove top.

"Then when their mother's second marriage failed, the girls were very upset. Kids need two parents."

"They're almost grown."

"Yes, they're growing up faster than I ever thought possible." Reid looked over at Megan. "I like having you here."

She smiled and came closer to put her arms around his waist from behind. "I don't think they like me."

"Not like you? How could that be? Of course they like you."

Laying her cheek against his back, Megan said, "I'm not so sure of that."

"Dad!"

Megan jumped away as if she had been caught at a crime, and she saw Terry glaring at her from the doorway.

"Yes, baby?" Reid said without turning around.

"The movie is starting. You'll miss the first part if you don't hurry."

"We'll be right there."

Terry gave Megan a long look of warning before she went back to the den.

"Maybe I should leave."

"And miss the movie? It's one you said you wanted to see."

She couldn't insist without giving Reid some reason, so Megan went with him into the den. Reid turned the lights down and settled on the couch with her as Jeanette sprawled on the floor and Terry slouched in an armchair. The movie was a sizzling suspense-drama, but Megan thought it couldn't compare with the tension she felt when she was around Reid's daughters.

When the film was at last over, Megan stood and said, "It's been quite an evening, Reid, but I have to go now."

"So soon? What about those late shows you're always talking about? *Gentlemen Prefer Blondes* is on next."

"I really have to get home." To the girls she said, "Goodbye. Have a nice visit."

"Thank you," Jeanette said absently. Terry said nothing.

Reid walked her to the door and leaned his forearm on the jamb. "I'm glad you came over tonight." He caught her eyes. "Is something wrong?"

"No, no. That is, my mind is on a phone call I got yesterday."

"Oh?"

"It was from an editor friend of mine, Susan Parsons. She has a job now with *National Geographic*, and they're offering me an assignment."

"Hey, that's great!"

"I'd have to go to Africa."

"Terrific." Reid's deep voice wasn't so enthusiastic now. "Africa, huh?"

She drew a deep breath. "I'd be gone all winter. I think *National Geographic* is considering me for a permanent position."

"Is that right?" Now he wasn't enthusiastic at all.

"It would probably mean a permanent move, and there would definitely be lots of travel." She managed a smile. "They aren't doing any studies on native life in Boulder, Colorado."

"No. No, I can see that you'd have to travel."

"It's *National Geographic*!" she said as if he had disputed her claim. "To write for them would put me in a wonderful position. My career would be assured!"

He was silent.

"This is the sort of break I've always dreamed of. And I didn't even have to pursue it—it was offered to me out of the blue."

"I can see what an opportunity this is. Does that mean you're going to take it?"

"A month ago I'd have climbed through the telephone wires in my eagerness to accept. Now I don't know."

Reid looked at the door. "You shouldn't pass up a chance like this. It may never come again."

"Then you're saying you want me to take the assignment?"

"No, I didn't say that." He touched her hair and brushed it gently from her face.

"You think I shouldn't take it?"

"Megan, I can't make that decision for you. If you don't accept because I asked you to stay, you might always regret it."

She wondered what that was supposed to mean. Was she really only a friend to him, and no one special? Perversely she discarded all her determination to remain unencumbered emotionally. Reid was terribly important to her.

Reid stroked her velvety cheek and wished he had the right to ask her to stay, or to follow her to the ends of the earth if she refused. If he asked her to stay, however, what could he offer her that would compare with worldwide recognition and the attainment of her ultimate career goal? He was convinced he wasn't a good marriage risk, and he wouldn't demean Megan with the offer of anything less.

"Will you come back to Boulder occasionally?" he asked at last.

"I haven't decided if I'm going to accept the assignment. There's so much I have to consider."

"This is a bad time to try to sell a house. Maybe you could rent it."

"I wasn't thinking about the house," she said testily.

"Is there something else holding you here?" He held his breath as he waited for her answer.

"Maybe not. I had hoped there was, but I must have been mistaken."

Reid pulled her into his arms and rubbed his cheek against the dark cloud of her hair. "I don't want you to go," he said so softly he didn't think she could hear him.

Megan tensed and tilted her head up to look into his eyes. "What?"

"I said I don't want you to go. Not forever. Not even for the winter."

Breathlessly she whispered, "Why?"

For an answer he bent his head and kissed her deeply, lovingly. Megan felt her soul soar to meet his as her arms went around his shoulders. He crushed her to him in a way that spoke of his longing and his reluctance to let her go. As his lips moved over hers, his hands crept beneath her sweater to move over the warmth of her skin.

Megan murmured hungrily as her passion burgeoned into full-fledged need. She wanted him desperately. If she couldn't have him permanently, well, she would have to accept that. Love for him was spoken in her kiss as she threaded her fingers through his thick silver hair.

Reid's hands moved eagerly up her back and around to cup her breasts. The sheer lace of her bra did nothing to conceal the swollen buds from his seeking fingers. Waves of pleasure swept through Megan as he teased and pleased her.

She wanted nothing more than for him to take her then and there, his daughters be damned. Propriety had no place beside the urges he was awakening.

"Reid," she murmured in a shaken voice when he embraced her as if he would never let her go. "Are you asking me to stay?"

For a long time he was silent, and she felt his muscular frame tremble with his desire for her. At last he spoke in a low voice, his breath stirring in her hair. "Love is like a butterfly, darling. You can't grab it and hang on to it. A butterfly has to be free, without nets or cages."

"Does that mean you're telling me to go?" Anguish touched her voice and made it break.

"It means you have to be free to make your own choice, especially on something this important."

"I understand. At least I think I do." She looked up at his face, etched with painful longing in the moonlight.

"I want to say more, but I can't. The decision has to be yours."

"You could really give me up?"

"To see you go would wring the heart out of me, but yes. If you choose to leave, I won't make it difficult for you."

"And if I stay?"

"There are no promises." His words were harsh, as if he were fighting to say just the opposite.

"Because it would influence my decision?"

"You make it very difficult for me. Don't you know that?" His hand cupped her cheek, and his love for her harrowed his face.

Megan drew him down to her for another kiss. He wrapped his arms around her and lifted her off the ground, then let her slide sensuously down the length of his hard body. She returned his kiss with an answering passion that left them both shaken.

"Megan," he whispered as his eyes searched hers. "Megan." With great resolution, he gently pushed her away and opened the door. "When you decide, let me know."

"I will." Her voice was soft and sweetened by his kisses. "I'll decide soon."

He leaned toward her for a moment as if he wanted to say something else. Then he nodded and straightened. Megan watched him turn and step back into the house as she stood on the front walk. She wanted to sleep on this and look at it objectively, but she knew her decision was as good as made.

Chapter Six

Megan lay awake all night. By dawn she realized her decision to turn down the *National Geographic* assignment wasn't what had kept her awake all night. It was her quandary over her feelings about Reid. She wasn't sure how her decision would affect the real dilemma of what to do about him. As sunrise softened the shadows in her room to pearl and pale pink, Megan finally admitted that she loved him. This was not infatuation or mere physical desire that she felt. This was true love. Had it been anything less, she could have gone to Africa and never looked back.

She snuggled under the covers and considered this development. He might love her or he might not. Reid was too complex for her to be certain. Whatever the case, Megan planned to do her best to encourage him to love her. A glance at the clock assured her it was too early to do anything about it now. Later she could call Susan Parsons. With a sigh, she at last drifted into sleep.

When she woke up again, she called Susan, then Reid. "Good morning, Reid. Did I wake you?"

"No, I get up early. We've been playing tennis. The girls enjoyed your coming over last night."

I'll bet, Megan thought as she recalled the fiasco. "I hope they didn't feel I was barging in on their visit."

"No, not at all," he said quickly. "I'm glad you came over, too."

"I've been thinking about what you said about my not being fair toward the catalytic heater. Would you like to give it a try tonight? That is, if you can take tomorrow off. I was thinking of going up into the mountains for one last camp out."

"Are you serious? It's cold out there."

"We'll be warm in the tent. We'll have your infamous heater."

"I could get tomorrow off," he said thoughtfully. "I don't have anything too important scheduled. I haven't camped out in years."

"In your business, that's shameful. What time do you take the girls home?"

"About three o'clock."

"Great. I'll be over to get you at four. Bring warm clothes."

"I'll see you then. Megan, before you hang up...did you make a decision?"

"Yes, I did. We'll talk about it this afternoon."

"You aren't going to tell me now?"

"Nope."

"Sounds ominous."

"I guess that depends on your point of view. See you in a little while."

As Megan hung up, she smiled. Let him fret a bit longer. She didn't want to ease his mind until he had explored all the possibilities of losing her.

At four she drove to his house in the old four-wheel-drive pickup she used for treks into the mountainous back roads. When she pulled up in Reid's drive, he came out with a canvas knapsack and a new sleeping bag. Although he looked eager, faint circles under his eyes showed that he hadn't slept well the night before, either. Maybe he cared for her more than she thought, Megan reflected hopefully.

As she backed out of the drive and headed out of town, Reid said, "At the risk of sounding puritanical, what sort of sleeping arrangements do you have in mind?"

"I have a tent in the back. It's large enough to sleep four, so we'll have room to move around. You can sleep on the far side if you like."

Reid glanced at her. "Just buddies, huh?"

Megan shrugged and didn't answer. The mountains loomed nearer, their snow-covered peaks thrust toward the sky.

"The girls couldn't believe I was actually going camping. Jeanette is sure I'll freeze."

"You won't. We have that heater, remember?"

"Terry thinks we're out of our minds. There's a cold front coming through tomorrow."

"We'll be home by then."

Megan had a place in mind, and within an hour they were pulling into a deserted campground.

"There's no one else here," Reid said.

"Great. We can have our pick of the spots. Not many people go camping in the autumn on a weeknight. The ranger will be around soon to collect the camping fee. If not, I'll slide it under the office door." She chose a spot

beside the rushing river. Huge trees circled the table and
barbecue grill. Past the clearing was a view of ragged
mountaintops.

"Are you sure it's all right to be here? It's not closed
for the winter?"

"Not until the first snowfall. Here, help me spread
these insulated pads on the ground."

When the pads were down, Megan showed Reid how
to set up the tent. It was roomy, even with Megan's
sleeping bag spread decorously on one side and Reid's on
the other. He observed the arrangement thoughtfully but
said nothing. Megan put the catalytic heater in the middle of the tent and checked to be certain it had plenty of
fuel. The ground wasn't perfectly level, but it was as even
as any of the sites in the campground.

Reid lit charcoal in the grill, and soon they had ham-
burgers ready to eat. Megan brought out chips and dip,
along with two canned drinks.

As Reid ate, he said, "What is there about eating outside that makes food taste so good?"

"I don't know, but you sure cook a mean hamburger.
In return for the treat, I'll cook breakfast tomorrow."

"That's sounds fair."

When they finished, Reid dumped the paper plates and
scraps into the heavy-lidded trash container buried in the
ground, while Megan fastened the remainder of their
food in the cab of the pickup to keep it from bears and
other wildlife.

Hand in hand they walked along the river, ducking
under low limbs and climbing over fallen trees. "There's
something I want to show you," Megan said in a low
voice.

"Why are we whispering?"

"You'll see."

The evergreen trees gave way to a copse of aspen that shimmered like gold in the slight breeze. Farther on, the trees thinned, and Megan motioned for him to slow down and move as silently as possible. Then Megan stopped and nodded toward the clearing.

What had once been a low-lying meadow was now a beaver pond. Avenues of pewter water meandered among islands of topaz grasses. At intervals there were low dams of gnawed twigs and branches and the rounded tops of the beavers' dens in the middle of the pond. Tiny bugs glittering like black sequins swam through the still water, making arrow-shaped wakes. A bird took flight and was reflected in the mirrorlike surface. From far away came the calls of birds settling in for the night.

"Do you see them?" Megan whispered. "Over there, by that big pine."

Reid looked across the pond and at first saw nothing but trees. Then a slight movement drew his attention to five elk standing at the end of the clearing. Although the pond was between Reid and the majestic animals, the elk seemed quite close. Hesitantly the larger buck led his herd down to the water's edge.

"They're beautiful," Reid said in an awed voice.

"I've watched them for years. About this time of day they usually come down for a drink. They'll be moving farther down the mountain to their winter grounds soon. I had hoped they would still be here."

They watched as the elk finished drinking and meandered back toward the safety of the woods. "How can anyone shoot something so beautiful?" Reid mused.

"I've never understood it. Maybe hunters don't take time to really see them. Maybe they're just insensitive."

The elk melted back into the woods, and Megan smiled up at Reid. "I'm glad you feel the same way I do about them. If you had wished for a gun, I'd have been very disappointed.''

''I'm no hunter. What about the beavers? Any chance of seeing them?''

She shook her head. ''I've never even caught a glimpse of one. You can see where they've brought down trees,'' she said as she bent to show him a twig that had recently been cut, ''but they're too shy.''

She straightened to find Reid much closer than she had expected. His blue eyes were smoky with emotion. Quietly he reached out and touched her cheek. ''Why did you really want to go camping tonight?''

''I wanted to show you my world,'' she replied as his touch sparked a fire in her. ''I wanted you to see the elk and the beaver pond before snows closed the road.''

''That's the only reason?''

''What else?''

''It could be your way of saying goodbye.'' His voice sounded strained, and she saw he was tensing for her reply.

''I talked to Susan Parsons today—the editor I told you about.''

''I remember.'' His eyes searched her face for a clue. ''When do you leave?''

''Actually, I'm not going. I told her no.''

''No?''

''That's right.''

''What about the African assignment? You can't afford to turn down something like that. It could be the turning point of your career.''

''Yes, I can. I did.'' She turned to walk back toward camp.

''Megan! Are you sure? I mean, this is *National Geographic*.''

"Yes, I know."

"Why did you do it?" He caught her arm and pulled her around to face him.

"I don't want to go to Africa. Not now. And I don't want to move."

He studied her for a moment, as if trying to let her words sink in. Suddenly he pulled her to him and enveloped her in a bone-crushing hug. Megan held him tightly and buried her face against his coat.

"You're really not leaving?" he whispered into her hair.

She shook her head. "I'm not leaving."

"I worried all night," he said in a muffled voice. "I tried to convince myself that this was best, that you were certain to snap at this chance, that I could bear to lose you." He cupped her face in his hands and looked deeply into her eyes. "But I couldn't stand the thought of being without you."

"Would you have let me go?"

He nodded slowly. "I would never put my happiness before yours. If you had decided to go, I would not have said a word in protest."

"You should have. What if that were all I was waiting to hear?"

"I don't want to play games with you. Not over something so important. If you'd wanted to go, I wouldn't have made it difficult for you."

"I don't want to play games either."

"Megan, why are you staying?"

She paused. She wasn't sure he could handle this much honesty. "Leave all this?" she said lightly as she made a gesture that took in the sweep of mountains and forest. "For the privations of Africa?"

The sun was sinking fast, and only the highest mountains were rimmed with gold and rose. Long fingers of shadow stretched through the aspen, and the pond took on a leaden hue.

"We'd better get back to camp," she said. "It'll be dark soon."

Reid remained thoughtfully silent.

They followed the river back to the tent, and Megan lit a fire in a circle of stones. Folding a blanket, she spread it on the cold ground. Night sounds came from the encircling forest, and the bushes rattled as a scurrying chipmunk dashed through in search of food. The logs crackled and popped, sending sprays of golden sparks upward.

Reid sat beside her and poked at the fire with the end of a stick. "How do you like my girls?" he asked unexpectedly.

Megan glanced at him. "They're very pretty, very intelligent."

"But do you like them?"

"I think I want to like them more than they want to like me. Last night they seemed to resent my presence."

"I guess it's because of the divorce. They've become very possessive of me."

"They love you a great deal. I envy you, to tell the truth. My one regret is not having children of my own."

"There's still time."

"I'm past the age where I want to start raising a family. I should be preparing to be a grandparent."

He laughed. "Only if you had very precocious children. You're not even forty yet."

"Not quite." She tossed a pinecone into the flames and watched it blossom into a fire flower. "No, I no longer want to have a baby, though for years I ached for one. Now I'd rather have kids about the age of yours.''

"I like teenagers. Most people don't seem to, but I do.''

"How did the girls like me? Did they say?''

"Jeanette said you're pretty.'' He smiled at her. "She was right.''

"They don't like me, do they?''

"How can they tell? They've only seen you a couple of times. They're very jealous of my time right now. Pamela's second divorce was unsettling for them.''

"That must have been difficult.''

In silence they watched the flames slowly devouring the wood. Overhead the sky grew black, and the nearby trees were shrouded in a cloak of invisibility. After a while Reid said, "Are you sure you won't regret not going to Africa?''

"Yes, I'm sure. I've made the right choice.''

"You never said why you're staying. It can't really be for the scenery here; Africa is famous for it. Wildlife, too. What's the real reason?''

"You never told me why you lost sleep over my decision,'' she countered. "Why was that, Reid?''

He studied the dying fire as if the answer might somehow be found in the embers. "It's getting late. And cold. I think that cold front may be coming through tonight.''

"Maybe you should light the heater and get the tent warm. I'll make us some cocoa.'' She went to the truck and got out two envelopes of instant cocoa and two Styrofoam cups. She smiled as she poured water into a pan and set the pan on the hot coals. The early arrival of the cold front was a bonus she hadn't expected.

Reid came out of the tent, leaving the flap partially unzipped to let air in for the heater. "It's not too easy to light, is it?''

"Not very."

"The tent will be warm soon."

Megan smiled again and poured hot water into the cups. "This will warm us up."

"It's good! I had almost forgotten how good hot chocolate can be on a cold night."

"You've forgotten how to play," she observed. "You're a success in every way, but in becoming one, you forgot how to enjoy the little things."

"I wouldn't say I'm such an unqualified success. I'm divorced, you know."

"That means the marriage failed, not you."

"I'm not good husband material," he told her again.

"Who told you such a silly thing? Pamela? She's hardly an unbiased observer."

"Still, she ought to know."

"In some ways people are like chameleons. I'm not the same with you as I was with, say, Hugh or Susan. You aren't the same with me as you are with your girls or Chad Merrick. Or Pamela. The fact that one combination isn't successful doesn't mean they'll all be that way. One of the happiest couples I know were each miserable with their first spouses."

"How were you different with Hugh?"

"At first I was more dependent. I was taught as a child that the man was head of the family. As Hugh became sick, I learned to be strong. By the time he was in a wheelchair, I was the head of the house, and I think he resented me for it."

Reid looked at her in surprise. "I thought you had the perfect marriage."

"We were happy," she said after a pause, "but maybe not as happy as I prefer to believe. We all tend to idealize the dead."

"Sometimes that makes it hard on the living. How can you expect a man to be as perfect as a memory?"

"My memories are more realistic these days. I don't want my man to be perfect. If he were, he wouldn't want me."

The fire sputtered and died down to a mere glow. Megan shivered. "I think you're right about that cold front. Ready for bed?"

Reid nodded and drew a deep breath as he looked at her beside the fire. He wasn't at all sure he could handle sleeping in a tent so close to her without touching her. Maybe she could remain platonic toward him, but he felt as if he were on fire every time she looked at him.

During the long night before, he had finally admitted something he had fought for days. He loved her, and he wanted her with him forever. His love for her was so great that he could have let her go if that would have made her happy. He still felt a bit weak from relief that she wasn't going to leave him. In his way had he been afraid, as Megan was, of loving someone and losing her? After all, Pamela had left him for another man, and she had done it with no warning at all. For a while he had felt as bereaved as if she had died.

He found a shovel in the truck and scooped dirt over the coals until the fire was smothered and only the flickering kerosene lantern lit the darkness.

Carrying the lantern, he followed her into the tent and adjusted the flap so that fresh air would replenish the oxygen used by the heater. "This tent is barely warmer than outside."

"It's not the tent that's at fault. It's the heater. That's what I tried to tell you. It doesn't work properly."

With a frown he knelt and turned the knob, but it was up all the way. "It works fine in the laboratory."

"On a perfectly flat surface. Yes, I know. Unfortunately, there are no perfectly flat surfaces here."

Reid tilted the heater, and the glow faded from the wire mesh. "It's a safety feature. If it's knocked over, it's supposed to go out." He found the box of matches and strained to get the tip of the flame through a tiny opening to relight the heater.

Megan unzipped her coat and laid it on the tent's canvas floor. "We won't freeze. It will keep us that warm." As if she were in the privacy of her own bedroom, she pulled off her bulky red sweater and tossed it onto her coat.

Reid did a double take when he saw she was wearing a tight peach-colored T-shirt and no bra. With her ample bosom straining against the soft knit, he could see the hard buds of her nipples. Her jeans were tight and fit her like a denim skin. As he watched, she unsnapped the waistband.

"What are you doing?" he managed to ask.

"Going to bed." She looked at him innocently. "I don't know why, but it's warmer to sleep without so many clothes."

"Oh." Reid turned away and moved the few feet to his own sleeping bag. He pulled off his coat and his white fisherman knit sweater and tossed them into the corner.

"Don't turn around," he heard her say. He froze as the sound of a zipper broke the strained silence. He couldn't have moved if he had to. The rustle of a sleeping bag told him she was under the covers. To his surprise his hands were shaking and he was holding his breath.

"Aren't you going to take your jeans off?"

"No." He yanked open his sleeping bag and lay down. Without his sweater, his bare skin felt as if it were freezing. "Are you sure this is warmer?"

"You'd be more comfortable without your jeans."

"No, I wouldn't."

"Suit yourself." She rolled over and reached her slender arm out to turn off the lantern. The only light was the dull red glow from the struggling heater.

Reid closed his eyes, but all he could see were her lovely breasts, straining to burst free from that tight T-shirt. Her jeans were on her coat. What was she wearing? Thermal underwear? He doubted it.

In the near darkness he heard her move, and all his senses were alert. What was she wearing? "Are you cold?" he asked.

"Freezing."

"Maybe we should go back to town."

"And miss the sunrise up here? Wait until you see it! The snowy peaks turn all the shades of an opal as the sun comes up." She was quiet for a minute. "Are you cold?"

"All the way through to my bones."

"We could put our sleeping bags together. We'd be warmer then."

Both held their breaths as each waited for the other to respond.

"Of course if you'd rather not . . ."

"It would be warmer," he said.

"Bring yours over here."

He saw her roll out of her bag and kneel as she unzipped it and spread it out flat. Her curved legs were bare, as were her hips. She wore silky bikini panties that left scarcely anything to the imagination. Reid stared at her. Didn't she realize what she was doing to him?

Megan looked at him, her lips parted slightly in the dim light. "Are you coming over here?"

He grabbed his sleeping bag and went to her. Trying not to look at the way her unrestrained breasts moved, he helped her fit the zippers together to form one large bag. Doubtfully he asked, "Is it really warmer without jeans?"

"Absolutely." She slipped into the flannel bed and pulled a blanket over it. Her dark hair spread over the pillow, and she looked as cuddly and sexy as any woman he had ever imagined.

Hastily Reid slipped off his jeans and slid into the sleeping bag. He noticed she was being awfully quiet all of a sudden. He moved slightly, and his bare leg touched hers. "Megan, this isn't going to work."

"Why not?"

"Why do you think? I can't lie next to you with practically no clothes on and simply go to sleep." His voice held an edge of exasperation.

"I know," she replied.

He rolled over to face her and found her eyes sparkling with repressed laughter. She shrugged as she bit her lower lip to keep from laughing.

"What about this vow to be honest with each other?"

"This is as honest as I could be. What did you want, an engraved invitation?"

He propped himself up on one elbow and touched her glossy hair. "Megan, I don't want to have an affair with you."

Disappointment flickered over her face, and she turned her head away. "I guess I...Damn! I'm not very good at this. I thought..."

"I want something more permanent. Megan, I love you."

She turned back to him, her face incredulous.

"I don't know what I'm offering you. I don't want another divorce, so I have to be sure. This has all happened so fast." He smoothed her cheek and felt the pulse race in the curve of her throat. "I'm not ready yet to propose marriage. Until I am, I was trying to keep away from your bed. I . . ."

"I love you."

The silence tingled between them as Reid let the soft words enfold him. "You love me?"

"And I think your idea of our remaining just friends is the most unlikely one I've ever heard."

"You do, do you?" He grinned.

"Absolutely. I love you; you love me." She smiled at the novelty of the words on her lips. "I want you, Reid. I want to make love with you. How will we know if it will last if we keep each other at arm's length?"

"What if we become lovers and one or the other falls out of love?"

"We love each other; therefore, we're already committed to some extent," she murmured. "There are never any guarantees."

"I don't ever want to hurt you."

"You never will."

Gently he bent to kiss her and felt her lips open beneath his as her thinly clad breasts grazed his chest. Reid's breath lodged in his throat as he pulled her to arch against him, and she returned his kiss with growing ardor.

He ran his hand beneath the thin fabric of her shirt and found her breasts. Taking a nipple between his thumb and forefinger he teasingly rolled it into a tighter bead. Megan murmured with pleasure as she returned his caress.

"Reid," she whispered. "I love you so."

He pulled the T-shirt over her head and tossed it aside. Drawing back, he admired her in the heater's dim red glow. "You're beautiful. I never thought you'd be so beautiful."

She ran her fingers over the hard muscles of his chest and shoulders. "I never knew you were built like a Greek god, either. This is a night of surprises."

He laughed softly. "I'm glad you're my woman."

She smiled as happy tears gathered in her eyes. Reid's words made her feel special, not as if she were a possession. "I would rather be your woman than anyone else's wife."

"Anyone?"

"Anyone," she repeated firmly. "I've never loved anyone the way I love you."

"Megan. My Megan."

Again he kissed her, and Megan felt the smooth planes of his muscles beneath her hands. The touch of her breasts against his chest thrilled her, and she pressed herself hungrily against him. "I love you."

Reid lowered his head and took a nipple into his mouth. Megan arched to give him better access, to offer herself more fully. Fire seemed to race through her and center deep within her. A hunger she had long denied burst forth and demanded satisfaction.

With unsteady fingers she removed his briefs and ran her hands over the hard curve of his buttocks as she felt the overwhelming sensation of his hot manhood pressed against her. She lifted her hips as he stroked away her panties and savored for the first time the long kiss of their bodies touching with no barriers at all.

She moved eagerly against him, but Reid said, "I want to make this last, darling. Our first time should be one you remember forever."

He kissed her deeply, causing all her passions to ignite, and his skillful fingers summoned sensations she had half forgotten and some she had never known. He seemed to know exactly how to touch her and where in order to bring her ever greater pleasure. Megan was aware only of his lips as they moved over her body, of his fingers that seemed determined to memorize every inch of her.

Nor did he repress her own explorations. Megan ran the tip of her tongue over his smooth chest and flicked the hard button of his nipple. Reid responded by drawing her own bud deep into his mouth and then raking it gently with his teeth as his fingers probed and enjoyed her most tender recesses.

The world seemed to dissolve until there was only Reid loving her and her loving him. Megan had the incredible sensation of her mind meeting his and merging so that she felt his pleasure and he was part of hers.

When at last he became one with her, Megan murmured in ecstasy. He filled her completely, and his every move sent tremors of delight through her. In unison they moved in the ageless dance of love. Higher and higher they spiraled on wings of passion. Megan felt herself reaching her completion, but she held back for as long as she could to prolong the exquisite pleasure. Then with a cry she reached the pinnacle and soared into ecstasy.

Reid's satisfaction was triggered by her own, and he held her tightly as they were rocked by the deepest fulfillment they had ever known.

"I love you," he said in a husky voice when finally she lay quietly in his arms. "I never knew I could love anyone the way I love you."

"I told you it would be warmer without our clothes," she murmured happily. Then she added mischievously, "It will be even warmer after I run out to the truck and get the other heater."

"What other heater?"

"The competition. The one that really works."

"You have another heater out there? What if I hadn't come over here? Would you have let us freeze to prove your point?"

"Reid, there wasn't a chance in this world that we wouldn't have ended up just like this."

He laughed softly. "You're a cagey lady, Megan."

"I know what I want. And I want you."

He held her close and let love wash over him. For the first time in his life, Reid felt complete.

Chapter Seven

Megan was determined to learn to like Reid's daughters. She had always made friends easily, and she saw no reason Terry and Jeanette should be exceptions. Reid obviously adored them, and since she and Reid loved each other, Megan was certain she could love his children. She simply didn't know them well enough yet.

All week Megan asked Reid about the girls' likes and dislikes, their special interests. She researched them as thoroughly as she would have the subject of an in-depth article. By Saturday she felt she knew them as well as anyone could by secondhand information.

"Don't be so nervous," Reid said as he watched Megan pace in his living room.

"I want them to like me. So much depends on these first few visits." She glanced at her watch. "They're late."

"That's Pamela for you. I should have gone to pick them up. Come here." He reached out to catch her wrist and pulled her into his lap. "As much as we love each other, this will all work out."

Megan sighed and touched her forehead to his. "I guess so."

"This past week has been the best one of my life," he said as he kissed the warm hollow of her neck. "I haven't been able to concentrate much at work, but my evening hours have certainly improved."

"You aren't tired of me yet?" she asked with a smile.

"I can't imagine ever getting tired of you." His blue eyes took on the dusky tones she now associated with their lovemaking.

"Look at me like that, and you may not be able to go to the door."

"Promise?"

"Look. A car just turned into your drive. It's the girls. Is that Pamela coming in with them?"

Reid shifted to look out the window. "Damn," he muttered. "It's Pamela, all right. I wonder what she wants now."

Megan slid off his lap and smoothed her blouse as he went to open the door. She heard a glad chorus as the girls hugged Reid. A short blond woman breezed by him and walked into the living room.

"Hello," Megan said.

"Reid, I didn't know you had company," Pamela said as she gave Megan a critical appraisal.

Reid looked at her suspiciously, then introduced them. "Megan, this is Pamela."

"Megan. The name is familiar."

"I met some of your friends at the Merricks' party."

"Oh, yes. I remember now." Again Pamela swept her gray eyes over Megan from head to toe. "We must talk sometime."

"All right." Megan wondered what she and Pamela could possibly have to say to each other, but this wasn't the time to ask.

"Reid, I want to ask you about my car insurance. Jack Riddley says the company won't cover that dent in my fender, but I could have sworn they would. Could you look over my policy and explain it to me?" She batted her eyes as if she found it all too complex to comprehend.

"No. Jack is your insurance agent. Ask him to explain it."

"Have you been in a wreck?" Megan asked.

"A minor one. My doctor is still watching me very carefully for signs of whiplash."

"I'm sorry to hear that."

To Reid, Pamela said, "Jack doesn't explain things in a way I can understand. You've always been able to say things so I can see what you mean."

"If Jack can't do it, ask Jim Buckner. Chad says you're dating him."

Again Pamela's heavily mascaraed eyelashes fluttered. "I didn't know you were checking up on me, Reid. What did Chad tell you?"

"I'm not checking up on you," he said in an exasperated tone. "He just mentioned it."

"Chad is such a gossip," Pamela said to Megan.

"Dad, can I have a soda?" Jeanette asked.

"May I," Pamela automatically corrected.

"I'll get it for you," Megan offered.

"I can get it myself."

Pamela raised her eyebrows at Megan's suggestion, and Megan felt surprisingly embarrassed. She shouldn't have

admitted such familiarity with Reid's apartment in front
of his ex-wife, she realized. Then she wondered why not.

Pamela gave her the same reproving look that she
might have shown an intruder. "Reid, may I speak to you
for a moment? Alone?"

His mouth was a grim line, but he stepped out onto the
porch with her.

"How's school?" Megan asked Terry.

"Same as always. Why do grownups always ask that?"

"I guess because we want to make conversation and
don't know what else to say."

"I never make idle conversation. I read that words are
tools and weapons, and I've decided they must never be
used lightly. I'm building character that will be invalu-
able in my career as an actress."

"What do you think about the political situation in
Iran?" Megan asked wryly.

"I'm going to go get a soda."

Megan watched her go, then sat on the arm of a chair.
Without any noise in the room, she could hear the conversation on the porch.

"No, she isn't living here!" Reid was saying, his words
clipped and angry. "Even if she were, it's none of your
business."

"But the girls! I can't leave them here if you two are
carrying on under their very noses."

"You must know I wouldn't do such a thing."

"All the same, I think the girls had better come back
home."

"No way."

"You saw them only last weekend, Reid. The divorce
decree says your visitation is every other weekend."

Megan got up to leave the room before she could hear
more. However, Reid had opened the door, and she

couldn't go into the other room without seeming to have been eavesdropping.

"You see them every day," Reid snapped. "I see them twice a month unless you want them out from under your feet!"

"That's not fair!"

"To make them leave now would be disappointing for them."

"Bring them home tonight," Pamela demanded. "Before they can see ... anything."

Reid's reply was mercifully muffled, but Megan saw Pamela hurry toward her car as he strode into the apartment.

"Did you hear that?" he asked heatedly.

"Well ... that is ... not on purpose."

"She thinks we're making out in front of the girls!"

"No, no," Megan soothed. "I don't believe that. Otherwise she wouldn't have left them here. I think she had their best interests in mind. After all, if I were their mother, I'd want to be sure about what my children were exposed to. She was just mistaken."

"She knows me better than to ever think I'd put the girls in an awkward situation!"

"You both overreacted. Let's forget it." Megan smiled, feeling as beatific as a saint. She could at least act as a pacifier in what was so clearly a misunderstanding.

Jeanette came in with a soft drink. "Is Mom gone?"

"Yes," Reid snapped.

Terry also had a drink. "Let's do something," she suggested as she came through the door.

"I know," Megan said brightly. "Let's go to Estes Park and shop."

"You're going, too?" Terry asked.

"There are plenty of stores here," Reid said.

"I know, but this will be fun."

"Mom's birthday is next week," Jeanette said. "We could shop for her gift in that store she likes so well. Remember, Dad?"

Megan faltered but was determined to keep up the goodwill. "Of course we can."

Terry pouted slightly. "I wanted to watch the rock station on TV. Our cable is out, and we can't get it at home."

"You can listen to the radio on the way," Megan suggested.

"Since when do you make all the decisions?"

"Terry!" Reid scolded.

"That's all right. I can see how Terry feels." Megan felt her saintliness beginning to fray.

"I like Estes Park," Jeanette said. "I think it's a good idea. Can we go, Dad?"

"Sure. Why not?" As the girls went out to the car, he said to Megan, "Are you sure you know what you're doing? Rock music all the way to Estes Park?"

"That's exactly what our parents said about our music, and it wasn't so bad. Besides, it's not all that far."

By the time they reached Estes Park, Megan's ears were ringing and she was longing for a song with lyrics she could repeat. Reid gave her an I-told-you-so look as he snapped off the radio.

They went up the steps to the small shopping mall that had been built into a hillside. A man-made stream ran down through the several levels of shops and boardwalks and splashed over stones and strategically placed treetrunks, helping to blend the businesses in with the natural beauty of the surroundings. Reid took Megan's hand and squeezed it lovingly as they followed the girls from shop to shop.

"I love it here," Jeanette gushed. "I'm so glad you suggested it, Megan."

Terry poked her sister in the ribs and gave her a warning glance.

"I'm glad you're enjoying it. Would you girls like some hot cocoa?"

"We're not babies," Terry snorted. "Hot cocoa!"

"How about a shot of bourbon then?" Megan suggested in a sugary tone. Sainthood was wearing thin indeed. Fortunately, Reid seemed not to have heard her.

"Look," Terry said, pointing to a window. "Let's get Mom some more of those wooden spice containers. Remember, Dad? You gave her some on your last anniversary."

"Did you buy them here?" Jeanette asked.

"Of course, dummy. Don't you remember driving up here and how we all sang on the way up and back?"

"You sang," Reid corrected. "I drove."

Megan's heart sank with the awareness that she had inadvertently led them on to yet another blissful memory. Forcing herself to speak, Megan said, "The spice holders are very pretty. I think they would be nice, Jeanette."

She watched the girls sort through the square wooden spice jars and wondered how she would ever get through to them. "The Brady Bunch didn't seem to have this problem," she whispered to Reid.

"The Brady Bunch is fiction."

"Do you think they'll ever accept me?"

"Of course. Jeanette said you had a good idea, remember?"

"I could learn to detest that word."

"You can't blame them for their memories."

"No, but they seem to recall only the happy times." She cut herself off. "Now I'm being silly," she scolded herself. "It's better that they remember the good times instead of being caught up in the misery they must have been feeling."

Reid nodded.

"There was misery, wasn't there? Arguments, things like that?"

"A few. Still, I was stunned when Pamela left. We hadn't been close, but I had no idea she was seeing someone else."

Somehow this admission hurt Megan more than the girls' trips down memory lane did. "I assumed everyone fought before getting a divorce."

"We've fought quite a bit since then."

Megan picked up a replica of a small church with stained-glass windows and pretended to study it with keen interest so that her feelings wouldn't show. She hadn't realized how difficult all this would be. "Some divorces don't seem to take as well as others."

"It took—I guarantee that. You don't hear me reliving the glowing memories. They remember singing; I remember us sitting in stony silence while the girls sang. Let them recall it inaccurately if it helps them. I don't care, and it changes nothing."

"You must think I'm a jealous witch." She replaced the church on the shelf.

"No, I don't."

"You should. It's true."

"Honey, you're trying too hard. Just relax and let the girls get to know you and vice versa. They've never met the Megan I know."

She smiled. "Pamela's afraid they have."

"I knew you could still smile."

"I thought I had been."

"Mostly you've looked intense or blank."

So much for sainthood, Megan thought.

"Dad, does Mom have the ones for nutmeg and all-spice?"

"I don't know."

Megan ignored the shopkeeper's frankly curious glance.

"Let's get these. Dad, are you buying her anything?"

"No." The shopkeeper gave them another look.

"But it's her birthday. She's thirty-three."

Megan's spirits lowered. No wonder Pamela looked so young.

"She's thirty-seven," Reid corrected Terry.

"See? I knew you remembered." Terry looked as pleased as if Reid had bought a gift after all. "How old are you, Megan?"

"Terry, that's enough." Reid's voice was sharp.

"I just wondered."

"You must have married young," Megan observed as Terry paid for the spice holders.

"Do we have to keep talking about her?"

"Sorry. Would you like some cocoa?"

"As a matter of fact, I would."

They went up a flight of steps and down a boardwalk to a small café. The girls sat at a table for two near the back, and Reid led Megan to a table by the window. She gazed out at the frantically splashing stream as she said, "I never knew how difficult it could be to fit two lives together. It's as if we're each dragging a puzzle piece behind us. The pieces seem to match, but we have to work at finding the right combination."

"Is it really that difficult?"

"I have only me to fit into the space. You have yourself, your daughters and what's-her-name."

"It's not easy for me to know you were so happily married, either. At least you know I choose to be separated from Pamela."

"I suppose so, but Hugh isn't a flesh-and-blood reminder to you."

"Megan, what's the matter with you?" He took her hand across the table and leaned forward as if he were ready to battle any dragon for her.

"I don't know. I've never felt like this," she said miserably. "Ever since I met you it's as if my emotions were riding on a yo-yo. I've never been so happy or so confused or so jealous. I've never been jealous in my entire life! And now look at me."

"I've been a bad influence on you?"

"You've been a wonderfully bad influence."

"Actually I rather like knowing you care enough to be jealous."

She frowned at him.

"But it's unfounded," he assured her.

"If I weren't around, would you go back to Pamela? Terry seems so certain that you would."

He laughed softly. "Terry has always had an overactive imagination." He stroked his thumb over her palm and curled her fingers under his. "I'm where I want to be and with the woman I love."

"I love you, too."

"We'll work this out. At least Jeanette is coming around."

Megan glanced at the girls' table and found Jeanette scowling at their touching hands. Megan drew her hand back and down into her lap. Reid was certainly optimistic.

On the way home Terry was filled to overflowing with memories and enthusiastically planned where the new spice holders should be placed in her mother's kitchen. Jeanette was silent, but Megan could feel a prickling on her neck as if the girl were still glaring at her.

"Are you taking us home?" Terry asked.

"How did you know your mother said for me to bring you back tonight?" Reid asked.

"I told her about Megan, and she said she would."

"What did you say about me?" Megan asked.

"Only that you're around a lot. It's true."

"Mom didn't like it," Jeanette added.

"That's tough," Reid replied. "Megan will be around for a long time. Your mother will have to get used to it."

The silence in the car grew strained, and after several miles Terry said stiffly, "I think you should take us home."

"Yeah," Jeanette echoed.

Without a word Reid drove to Pamela's house and waited for his daughters to get out. "Bye, Dad," Jeanette said.

"Goodbye, Father," Terry said in a bereaved tone.

"Good night, Jeanette, Terry. I'll call you tomorrow."

"Goodbye," Megan called out as they walked across the yard. "I guess they didn't hear me," she said to Reid.

"Probably not."

"I'm so sorry it turned out this way."

"Everything will work out. You'll see. A few years from now we'll look back on this and laugh." He looked as if he didn't believe that any more than she did.

"Will I be around in a few years?"

"That's up to you."

Megan reached out and put her hand on his thigh. "That sounds rather permanent."

"Megan, move in with me."

"What?"

"We've been together every night this week. There's no reason for us to keep going from your house to my apartment. We love each other. Why not live together?"

"What if it doesn't last? Besides, I couldn't possibly fit all my things into your apartment." She sighed. "Not only that, but Pamela won't let the girls come over if I'm living there."

"She has to. I have visitation rights. As for its not lasting, when has there ever been a guarantee that any relationship will last? You're the one who told me that, if you'll recall."

Megan slowly shook her head. "Your daughters would never accept me as a live-in girlfriend. Girlfriend! I hate that term, but there isn't one that fits."

"How about life-partner?"

"How about mistress, or to give it an exotic ring, le-man? No, Terry and Jeanette would never accept that."

"This is between us."

"It's between them, too. It has to be. Don't you see that?"

"Yes, I guess I do," he said reluctantly. "I just don't want to admit it. Hell, I'm forty years old. Can't I live with a woman if I choose? Megan, there's something wrong here."

"No, there's not," she answered. "We don't have un-limited freedom. Everything has its consequence. I just don't choose the result of our living together."

Reid was quiet until they pulled into his parking space. "I can't ask you to marry me, Megan. Not yet."

"I wasn't hinting that you should."

"I'm not sure I can succeed at marriage. From all I've seen, it's just a string of broken appliances, hair in curlers and cold shoulders."

"Not always."

"Now who's making whom jealous?"

She sighed and shook her head. "I wasn't referring to Hugh."

"Let's go inside. The night is still young. I don't have to be in the office until nearly noon."

"For a man who was so absorbed in his work, you seem to be changing."

"I used to be afraid to slack off in any way. I made my sporting-goods stores and the equipment line from the ground up. I've always been afraid everything would fall apart if I loosened my grip even a little."

"And has it?"

"Not a bit." He put his arm around her shoulders as they walked to the door. "You see, I'm also a man with a one-track mind. I see a goal, and I move forward relentlessly. Right now you're my goal."

"I see," she said with a smile. "I also see where Terry gets her flair for the dramatic. Tell me, Mr. Spencer, where does your present momentum seem to be taking you?"

"That remains to be seen, Ms. Wayne. However, I might say this: I may be prejudiced against marriage, but I have no qualms about practicing some of the tenets."

"Who knows? Maybe the prejudice will go away some day and the practice will pay off."

" 'Step into my parlor, said the spider to the fly.' " He bowed to usher her into the apartment and gave her a leering grin.

The following Wednesday Megan answered her door-bell to find Pamela on the porch. After a pause, Megan said, "Come in. What brings you here?"

"It's taken me days to get up the courage to speak to you," Pamela said as she perched on the edge of the nearest chair and glanced nervously at the African tribal mask on the opposite wall. "We have to talk."

"Oh?" Megan curled into an overstuffed chair and wished she hadn't chosen this particular day to clean out the dusty attic.

"It's about Reid. The girls tell me that you're over there quite often."

"Yes, I am."

"Surely you can see what an adverse impact that has on them. They must, well, wonder."

"They know I don't live there. As you can see, I live here."

"These aren't young children who might overlook nuances. They're young ladies."

"Are you calling me to task? If so—"

"No, no. I wouldn't presume to do that. No, I was only saying that, well, you understand."

"Yes. I do. If that's all you came here to say, then—"

"There is one other thing. Reid and I, that is, we were in the process of reconciling when you entered the scene."

"Oh? That's not what he told me."

"Men!" Pamela shrugged in a way that was utterly feminine. "You know how they are. Reid wouldn't tell you the truth if he was . . . after something."

"I don't believe this."

"I'm sure it must be confusing. However, I need him. So do his daughters. I'm asking you to step back so our family can be reunited."

Megan stared at Pamela.

"I'm not the sturdy, efficient type you are. I need my husband."

"You mean your ex-husband."

Pamela pretended not to hear Megan and let her eyes fill with tears. "I miss him so much. You can't imagine."

"I understand you left him for someone else. That doesn't sound like deathless devotion to me."

"He told you that? Why would he say such a thing!" Pamela looked as if she were shocked beyond words. "I remarried, but it wasn't like that."

Megan didn't believe her, but she had the odd feeling that Pamela had begun to believe herself.

"You see, I can't manage without Reid. It's so difficult being a mother. Without him at home, I have to do it all."

"I know it's hard, but—"

"How could you possibly know? Have you ever had a baby? Do you know what it's like to worry about your children constantly and see to it that they grow up as perfectly as possible? To know your husband might come home if there were no one preventing him?"

Megan knew she was staring, but she hadn't seen a performance like this since the civic theater's last show. "I'm not stopping Reid. I have a feeling no one can sway him once he has his mind made up about something."

"You needn't tell me about him." Tears flowed down Pamela's cheeks. "I've lived with him since I was twenty."

"Except for the time with your second husband. Don't forget him."

"I know it must give you pleasure to make this as hard for me as possible. I expected no more. But please, please, consider what I've said."

"I doubt I'll ever forget it."

"The girls and I need him. I hate being alone and seeing them without a father."

"They have a father who loves them very much. As for it being difficult to manage alone, I know all about that."

Pamela shook her head as if she hadn't heard a word Megan said. "Life is so hard without him, and we were so close to making up. So very close."

"I've asked Reid about it, and he says the differences are irreconcilable."

"You can't believe that. I don't expect you to do it for my sake, but think of my poor children."

"They're practically adults themselves."

"Of course it seems that way to a woman who has never experienced motherhood, but believe me, it's very different to someone who has. I can still hear little Terry saying Mom-and-Dad as if it were one word. That's how they saw us—as if we were one. I guess you couldn't possibly understand that."

"You're right." To hear Pamela, one would think Terry and Jeanette were angelic toddlers and that Reid had left them only yesterday. Megan wouldn't have been surprised if Pamela suddenly launched into a recitation of the Victorian poem "Demon Rum."

"I'm...I'm having to go to work soon," Pamela confessed in a rush of tears. "The support the court ordered Reid to pay will be stopping soon, and it hardly covered my expenses, anyway."

"That's a shame," Megan said without conviction.

"The girls will have to come home to an empty house after school. They'll become latchkey children."

"That's too bad, but it can't be helped. It's an unfortunate sign of the times."

PLAY
SILHOUETTE'S

LUCKY HEARTS
GAME

AND YOU COULD GET

- ★ FREE BOOKS
- ★ A FREE UMBRELLA
- ★ A FREE SURPRISE GIFT
- ★ AND MUCH MORE

TURN THE PAGE AND
DEAL YOURSELF IN

PLAY "LUCKY HEARTS" AND YOU COULD GET...

★ Exciting Silhouette Special Edition® novels—FREE
★ A folding umbrella—FREE
★ A surprise mystery gift that will delight you—FREE

THEN CONTINUE YOUR LUCKY STREAK WITH A SWEETHEART OF A DEAL

When you return the postcard on the opposite page, we'll send you the books and gifts you qualify for, absolutely free! Then, you'll get 6 new Silhouette Special Edition novels every month, delivered right to your door months before they're available in stores. If you decide to keep them, you'll pay only $2.50 per book—25¢ less per book than the retail price—plus 69¢ postage and handling per shipment. You may return a shipment and cancel at any time.

★ Special Extras—Free!

You'll also get additional free gifts from time to time as a token of our appreciation for being a home subscriber.

FREE FOLDING UMBRELLA

You'll love this bright burgundy umbrella made of durable nylon. It folds to a compact 15" to fit into your bag or briefcase. And it could be YOURS FREE when you play "LUCKY HEARTS."

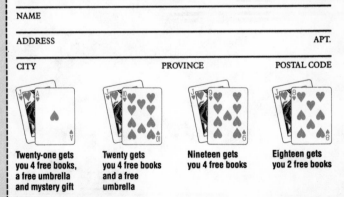

DETACH AND MAIL CARD TODAY

Business Reply Mail
No Postage Stamp
Necessary if Mailed
in Canada

Postage will be paid by

Silhouette Book Club
P.O. Box 609
Fort Erie, Ontario
L2A 9Z9

Canada Post
Postes Canada
125

"How can you be so heartless? I had hoped you would understand."

"I see that it's hard for you. My own life hasn't been a cinch, either. No one's is. If they'd like to, the girls can come here after school. I work at home."

"Never!" Pamela hissed as she bolted out of the chair. "Come here? Never!" She stalked to the door and yanked it open. "Then you won't quit seeing Reid?"

"It's about as likely as a snowball in hell," Megan said pleasantly.

Pamela flounced out to her car, and Megan closed the door behind her. In a way she was glad Pamela had come. She knew now that Reid was much better off without her and that Megan was better for him than Pamela would ever be. With a smile she put her jealousy into a closet of her mind and firmly closed the door.

Chapter Eight

At first Megan was aware only of the cold. It permeated her bones, and when she shivered she saw the snow and smelled the raw odor of newly turned dirt and the cloying scent of carnations. Megan frowned and burrowed deeper into the pillow without opening her eyes. The faint sound of the preacher's voice began softly but became louder and louder, the words indistinguishable and jumbled together. As much as she struggled to turn back, she was drawn to the mounded flowers beneath the dark green awning, and she felt the mourners staring at her. Willing herself not to look, yet unable to do otherwise, she turned to the flowers and what lay underneath, and she saw Hugh's flower-bedecked coffin hovering over the yawning grave. Overwhelming bereavement swept over her, making her panic and struggle to be free of the recurring nightmare.

With a strangled gasp Megan sat up, her body trembling and her throat constricted. For a minute she couldn't get her bearings. The windows and doors were all wrong. She looked around wildly.

"Megan? Megan, what's wrong?"

She jumped at the sound, and remembrance flooded over her. "Reid! I... The nightmare. I had a nightmare." She let him draw her into the warm safety of his arms, and she rubbed her cheek against the strength of his chest.

"Tell me about it." His deep voice was still fuzzy with sleep, but she knew he was awake and attentive to her.

"It's a nightmare I have over and over. I'm reliving Hugh's funeral, only the colors are too bright and the scent of flowers is too strong. Everything is simply too much to bear. And when I see the coffin, I..." She shuddered. "I used to dream it often in those first few months after he died."

"It's all over now, darling. You're safe."

"I know, but it's always so hard to shake it off. It's not like a dream where a monster is after you or where you're running from some unknown terror. This really happened—exactly as I dream it." She held Reid tightly and listened to the comforting thud of his heart. "Since I fell in love with you, the nightmare has come back."

"I don't have to be a psychiatrist to figure out why." He gently stroked her silky skin. "You're afraid of losing the one you love."

"Dumb, isn't it?"

"No. Especially when it's happened to you before."

"I didn't want to fall in love again. I really didn't!"

He was silent as he continued to comfort her.

"To love is to be vulnerable. I feel I have so much to lose now."

"Are you saying you want to pull back? To try to end our love?" He seemed to be holding his breath.

"No." Her voice was so soft that he could hardly hear her. "No, to leave you would be the same as losing you. I love you too much."

Reid rolled over so that he was gazing down at her. "I'm glad to hear that. Darling, I'm not going anywhere, and nothing is going to happen to me. I love you. Nothing will come between us."

"You're sure of that?" She touched his faint stubble of morning beard.

"As sure as anyone can be."

"Make love with me," she whispered. "Love me."

He claimed her lips and threaded his fingers through her thick hair. Between kisses, he murmured, "Making love with you is always a pleasure."

She buried her face in the warm curve of his neck and kissed the steady pulse she found there. His body was hard and strong under her hands as she ran her fingers over his back and down the indention of his spine. Unlike the night before, his kisses were languorous and sensuous rather than hotly demanding. She enjoyed the many moods of their lovemaking.

His palm cupped her breast, and his fingers teased her nipple to eagerness as his kisses grew longer and more exciting. Megan drew herself farther beneath him so that her other breast flattened against his chest and she felt his rigid maleness against her thigh. She looped her leg around his to hold him close and returned his kisses with growing ardor.

"Reid," she whispered. "Reid."

His tongue traced the moistness of her lips and passed over the edges of her teeth as she met it with her own.

"I love the way you taste, the way you smell, the way you feel. I like waking up to find you here beside me."

"I like that, too."

"Move in with me, Megan. There's no reason to run back and forth like this."

"No."

"I'll move in with you, then."

"We can't do that, either."

He sighed and gazed in loving exasperation into her face. "You're no more likely to lose me if we lived together than you are as it is."

"What's the difference in living together and being married? Both are commitments," she countered. "I'm not the only one with those hang-ups."

"I know. I've been thinking about that." He left a trail of kisses from her temple down to her throat. "I've thought about it a lot."

He felt the incredibly soft texture of her breast and how her nipple beaded against his palm. Sliding his hand lower, he passed the gentle rise and fall of her rib cage and the valley of her waist that rounded into her hips. "You're so soft. Your skin is like velvet."

"I love for you to touch me, to feel your body lying upon mine."

He cupped her buttocks and pulled her against him firmly. She was small and compact but not fragile. One squeeze wouldn't snap her in half, yet she was utterly feminine. Moving his hand over her thigh, he eased her legs open and lay in her enticing nearness for a few tantalizing moments before slowly becoming one with her.

Megan murmured in delight and buried her face against his shoulder as she felt him fill her. Warmth from him spread all through her, and she remained very still, savoring the sensation. After a moment she began to move, and he took up her rhythm.

Excitement grew in her, and passion began to replace mere pleasure. She wanted him. She needed him in an elemental way that was honed and refined by love. As his strokes became deeper and more demanding, she kept pace with him. A spark kindled deep in her loins and turned her blood to fire. Higher and higher she seemed to spiral as Reid stoked the flames to a roaring inferno.

All at once she reached her peak and cried out as waves of sheer delight thundered through her. Within moments she felt Reid thrust deeply with his fulfillment, and he murmured her name as they held each other tightly. The universe around them was nonexistent; they alone were real. Love encompassed them and prolonged the satisfaction of their completion.

Slowly, piece by piece, Megan became aware of the bed and the room and the sound of raindrops pattering against the windowpane.

"It's tempting," she whispered. "Very, very tempting to say yes and move in here."

"I want to come home at night and find you here and wake up every morning with you by my side."

Megan smiled and stroked his cheek. "I even like the way you have a bit of a beard in the morning and how your hair gets all tousled from sleep."

"I like everything about you."

"I don't think I'd even mind cooking for you—and goodness knows I'm not terribly domestic."

"I'm not looking for a cook. I love you so much that I'd even repair your appliances," he bargained with a grin.

"I can repair my own. Can you cook?"

"We could eat out often." His eyes grew serious. "Does that mean you're considering moving in here?"

"Maybe. But it makes more sense for you to move in with me, if we agree to do this."

"I wouldn't mind that."

"What about the commitment? If we agree to live together, I want to know it's long term. Think about it, Reid. Don't decide too quickly. I don't want us to move too fast or too irrevocably. What if you overdose on me and tire of me in a month?"

"The only burnout we're likely to have with each other is spontaneous combustion. I can't get enough of you."

"All the same, if you see me every day and every night, you might change your mind."

"Or you might change yours?"

"No. When I love, I don't love lightly."

"Nor do I," he said gently.

"I'll consider it."

"So will I. You know it would be more difficult with the girls if I move to your house."

"Still, there's more room there. We wouldn't be crowded." She thought for a minute. "How would they feel about it—if we move in with each other?"

"They're growing up. They'll understand. Regardless of what we decide, I think we should tell them how we feel about each other."

"Are you sure about that?"

"Of course. Then, if we do move in together, they won't be surprised."

"When and how do you plan to do this?"

"Tonight. We'll tell them tonight."

"So soon?"

"Why put it off? I'll call and tell them I want to see them and bring them over here. We can tell them together over dinner."

"All right," she said doubtfully.

"Once you see how happy they are for us, you'll know we'll have no problems."

Megan sighed and kissed his nose. "I love you."

"I love you, too. Don't look so worried."

Reid dialed Chad Merrick's number and sat back in his swivel chair while the phone rang. "Chad?" he said when his friend answered. "Let's meet for lunch." He glanced at his watch. "Sure, one o'clock is fine. At Parsley's? Sure. See you there."

He hung up and shuffled through the papers on his desk. Production was always slower this time of year, and he had very little that was pressing. Usually he worried about that and racked his brain from October to February over new ideas for the summer lines, just as he spent the rest of the year working on the ski equipment. Megan had showed him that it wasn't necessary for him to work every available hour of the day, and remarkably, he found he still accomplished just as much.

By the time he left for Parsley's he was well into his day's work and was feeling as if he were on top of the world. Chad was already there, and as soon as Reid joined him, he ordered his usual.

"What's up?" Chad asked when the waiter left. "You sounded strange on the phone."

"Strange? No, I sounded like a man in love."

"Who? Megan Wayne?"

"Chad, this is it. This is the one I've always been looking for."

"How do you know? You've only known her a short while." He studied his friend with concern.

"I know. That's the amazing part. It's as if I've known her for years. Forever! When I'm around her, I'm another person."

"I sort of liked the old one," he joked. Then he became more serious. "What do you mean, you're another person? In what way?"

"I'm more relaxed. I laugh a lot. We never run out of things to say to each other. Do you know what we did recently? We went camping."

"No!" Chad teased. "You? Get serious."

"We really did. And I enjoyed it!"

"Reid, this is going to come as a shock to you, but many people camp out, and most of them enjoy it. That's why your business makes so much money."

"I know, but I'd forgotten what it was like. I used to go camping when I was a kid, but I hadn't been in years. I'd forgotten how much fun it could be. Don't you see? It's Megan. She makes everything new and fresh for me. I've never met anyone quite like her."

"I commend you on your discovery."

"Chad, I'm serious. I love her, and she loves me."

Chad's grin faded, and he looked at his friend more closely. "You told her this?"

"Of course."

"Well, I guess you know what you're doing, but it seems awfully fast to me. Why, I never heard you mention her name until about a month ago."

"I didn't know her before then. Don't look at me like that. Sometimes it happens fast."

"This is close to the speed of light." He paused before saying, "Don't get me wrong. I liked her when I met her at the party at my house, and she seemed as if she would be a lot of fun to be with, but you're not just somebody off the street with an average job. You're worth over a million dollars."

"She's not like that," Reid protested instantly.

"Maybe not, but I'll bet you hadn't even thought of it until I pointed it out. After all, you're my best friend. I don't want to see you jump into a hasty marriage and then need me as a lawyer."

"No, I've told her I don't want to remarry, and she feels exactly the same way."

"That's good."

"So I've asked her to move in with me."

"What! Have you ever heard of common-law marriage? Palimony?"

"She hasn't agreed to it yet. She's still considering my offer. See? If she were after my money, she would have jumped at the chance. Do you know what she does for fun?"

"Goes camping?"

"And watches old movies and goes on picnics and takes walks in the woods. She's not interested in high living."

"People change after they're married. Look at Alice. For that matter, look at Pamela."

"I told you we aren't considering marriage."

Chad smiled. "I want you to be happy, Reid. That's why I'm playing devil's advocate. I see so many couples rush into something like this and then regret it when it comes time for the property settlement."

"I have my eyes wide open. Don't worry about that. After Pamela, I'm not looking for another wife. I just wanted you to know what's going on in my life these days." After a thoughtful pause, he added, "We're going to tell Jeanette and Terry tonight. They have a right to know how important Megan is to me.''

"Are you sure that's a good idea?''

"Well, we're not going to mention the part about living together. It may not come about, and there's no reason for them to know that yet. I just want them to know I love her and she loves me.''

"What is it about love that makes people go a little crazy and want to shout about that love from the rooftops?''

"Go ahead and scoff. But this is the real thing. You'll see.''

"Just don't rush into anything. If it's real, it will last. I'm saying that as your best friend.''

"I know you are. That's how I'm taking it. I know it seems fast, but we've spent a lot of time together since we met, and, well, you talked to her. Does she strike you as a fortune hunter?''

"No, not at all. I liked her a great deal.''

"There! You see, Chad. I know what I'm doing.'' He didn't blame Chad for being distrustful. That was just his way. His line of work tended to make him skeptical. Reid smiled to think what a different reaction he would get from his daughters.

Megan changed clothes three times before she was ready to go to Reid's. To ensure the success of the meal, she cooked it at home in her familiar kitchen. Feeling as if she were strolling into a bear's den, Megan loaded the casserole and salad into her car and drove the few blocks to his apartment. Her new key was shiny as she fit it into the lock. Reid wasn't home yet, and she felt odd being there without him.

To dispel her uneasiness, Megan bustled around, turning on lights against the approaching dusk and straightening the already neat magazines and potted plants. After glancing at her watch a dozen times and checking it against every clock in the apartment, she heard the sound of his car pull into the parking lot. Instantly her fingers grew icy and her stomach knotted. She had to remind herself to breathe.

Reid's key clicked in the door, and she heard the girls' happy voices behind him. Megan unclenched her hands and tried to smile normally. He came in, and his broad grin made her feel at home. "How was your day?" she asked as if this were all perfectly normal.

"Same as always."

"What's she doing here?" Terry demanded, stopping as if she had run into a wall.

Jeanette had smiled at Megan, but when she saw Terry's displeasure, her smile vanished abruptly.

"I've cooked dinner," Megan said with forced cheerfulness. "Girls, will you set the table?"

"Why is she telling us what to do?" Jeanette asked in a perfect imitation of Terry.

"Hey, where did that smile go?" Reid asked. To Megan he said, "Jeanette was just telling me that she made the honor roll at school."

"Why, that's wonderful!"

Jeanette's smile returned shyly. "I never made the honor roll before."

"Big deal." Terry went into the den, and Megan heard the television go on. "Come here, Jeanette. The show's starting."

"I'll set the table," Reid said.

"You don't have to. I should have already done it, but I thought the girls would feel more included if they helped."

"I want to." He kissed her lightly. "I also want you to know how much I enjoy coming home to you."

"Have you told them?"

"No. I thought we should do it together."

"Good idea. I hope you like this casserole. Do Jeanette and Terry like broccoli?"

"Sure."

Megan warmed the dish in the microwave and took the salad from the refrigerator. "I forgot to make a dessert."

"We don't need one."

"I forgot rolls, too."

"Quit being so nervous. You act as if you're about to confront dragons," he whispered.

"Aren't we?" she hissed back.

"We can eat bread. No one says we have to have rolls with dinner. Right? If all goes well, we'll go out for ice cream before we take the girls home."

"Ha! You're nervous, too!"

Reid didn't answer, but he kissed her forehead. "The microwave is finished."

When they were seated at the table, Megan tried to carry the conversation over the girls' silent, stony faces. Reid tried hard to act as if nothing at all were wrong.

"What's this green stuff?" Jeanette asked.

"It's not broccoli, is it? I hate broccoli," Terry put in.

"No, you don't," Reid insisted.

"Yes, I do."

"Try it, Terry. I think you'll like it," Megan said.

Terry took a slice of bread and looked at it suspiciously. "Are we having sandwiches? Where are the rolls?"

"Can I have a sandwich?" Jeanette asked.

"No. You two stop misbehaving and eat." Reid took a bite and chewed appreciatively. "This tastes great."

"Thanks."

Terry looked from one to the other. "What's going on here?"

"What do you mean?" Megan asked.

"You're both acting funny."

"We have something we want to tell you," Reid said.

"Uh-oh," Jeanette muttered.

"No, no. It's good news. Megan and I are, well, over the past few weeks..."

Megan gripped her fork so tightly that her knuckles turned white. "He means we've fallen in love."

A bomb would have caused less stir. Jeanette burst into loud tears, and Terry slammed down her fork and glared at them both. "Love!" she snorted. "You've got to be kidding!"

"I know this is a bit of a surprise..." Reid began.

"No, it's not! I was afraid of this! Well, don't expect me and Jeanette to say it's okay!"

"Terry, Reid and I don't—"

"You keep out of this! Everything was great until you came along!"

Jeanette's sobs increased, and she showed signs of becoming hysterical.

"Jeanette, stop it!" Reid ordered. "Terry, be quiet!"

"Sure, you want me to be quiet! That would suit you just fine, wouldn't it? Well, I won't! And neither will Jeanette!"

Megan stared at the girls in shock. She had expected a scene but nothing like this.

Reid's expression was thunderous. "Terry, I won't have you acting like this. You're my child, not my mother!"

"Does that mean you two are getting married? Does it?"

Reid and Megan exchanged a look.

"We haven't decided," Megan said through stiff lips.

"You'd just better not! I can tell you that. You'd better not. If you do, I'll run away forever!"

Jeanette's sobs became choking hiccups.

"Don't threaten me, Terry. Jeanette, stop that this minute!"

Megan stood up, her face pasty and her eyes dark with suppressed anger. Without a word, she went into the kitchen, shouldered the strap of her purse and hurried out into the night. She heard Reid call to her as she was running to her car, but by the time he dashed outside, she was spinning out of the parking lot.

A glaze of tears clouded Megan's vision, and she brushed them away. She was still shocked at Terry's outburst and Jeanette's tears, but fury was fast overwhelming her. "Those are the worst kids I've ever seen!" she ground out as she turned into her drive and slammed on the brakes. "They're terrible!"

She flounced into the house and slapped on the light switch as she threw her purse onto the kitchen table. Furiously she paced into the living room and turned on a light as she yelled, "I'm glad they're not mine!"

Feeling considerably better for having said it, she flopped down into a chair and stuck her feet out in front of her. She felt like a coward for running out on Reid, but if she had stayed, she would have said things that were best left unsaid.

"How did such a terrific man get such rotten kids?" she asked the ceiling. She picked up a small pillow and considered hurling it at the wall, but her anger was cooling. Megan's temper flared high, but once she let off steam, it calmed fast.

For an hour she sat in the chair and imagined all the biting things she wanted to say to the two girls, especially Terry. She had thought Jeanette was beginning to like her a little. She threw the pillow at the wall, and it hit with a satisfying thud.

As usual when she was angry, Megan felt hunger pangs seize her. She went into the kitchen and put together a bologna sandwich and grabbed a soft drink.

When the key turned in her lock, Megan jumped and wheeled to face Reid. He looked as bad as she felt, and she could only stare.

"May I come in?"

For an instant she hesitated, then said, "Sure. Do you want a sandwich?"

"At a time like this? I may never eat again." He closed the door and stood there looking at her. "Are you all right?"

"Yes, I'm just angry. Where are the girls?"

"I took them home after I chewed them out. Megan, I'm sorry about all this."

"It wasn't your fault."

"Yes, it was. I should have listened to you. We shouldn't have told them."

"It was a shock to them."

"More than I expected."

"Do they always act so bad?"

"Bad?"

"Well, you have to admit that was some tantrum they threw."

"They were naturally upset . . ."

"Upset! I've seen toddlers with more restraint!"

"Don't yell at me, Megan! You shouldn't have blurted it out like that!"

"What?"

"I needed time to prepare them!"

"Reid, they aren't Victorian baby dolls complete with fainting couches."

"They aren't truck drivers either. You just blurted it out, and that's what caused the problem!"

"Quit saying I blurted it out! I told them in a straightforward, honest way. If they chose to act like spoiled brats, that's not my fault."

"Spoiled brats? Don't you talk about my daughters like that!" He strode to her and glared down at her.

Megan slammed her sandwich onto the table, put her hands on her hips and glared back. "If they were my daughters, I'd turn them both over my knee! It seems to be long overdue!"

"That's a fine way for you to talk! Why is it the ones who have no children are always the experts?"

"That was a low blow," she hissed furiously.

"Quit telling me how bad my daughters are! That's pretty low, too!"

"Can you really not see they were putting on an act? World War lll wouldn't have caused such a reaction!"

"They're sensitive, caring children!"

"Bull! They're putting on a snow job that anybody ought to see through."

"Jeanette cried until she threw up! Does that make you feel better?"

"I felt like doing the same!" She made no move to back down and glared at him, nose to nose. "Is that something they learned from their mother?"

Reid's face went chalky white. A muscle in his jaw ridged, and his lips thinned in fury. Without a word he turned and stalked out.

Megan gripped the back of the chair and hoped she wouldn't be sick. She heard his car screech out of the drive and go down the street in a squeal of tires.

"Damn!" she burst out. "Damn, damn, damn!"

She was as angry at herself as she was at the girls. Reid had looked as if he never wanted to see her again. She ran her fingers shakily through her hair. What had she done? Did she really expect Reid to join her in running down his daughters? They might be spoiled, but he loved them. She could never ask him to choose between her and them.

Megan grabbed her purse and yanked out the keys. In seconds she was on her way back to Reid's house. As she turned the corner, she almost ran into him as he was heading back toward her house. She jerked to a stop by the curb and got out as he opened his car door.

For a long moment they stared at each other across the yards of pavement. "I'm sorry," they said in unison.

Megan took a tentative step forward. "I shouldn't have said those things. They were unforgivable."

"I got mad because they were true. Especially the part about them learning that from Pamela. I hate to see any of her in them."

Slowly they met in the middle of the street. "Can you forgive me, Reid?"

He drew her to him and held her in a bone-crushing embrace. "I was so afraid I had lost you! Of course I forgive you."

She drew back and said shakily, "Come home with me before we get run over."

Half an hour later they were sitting in Megan's kitchen, finishing off their sandwiches and some onion dip. "This sure isn't the way I planned this evening," Megan said as she drained her soft drink.

"You can say that again."

"Want another sandwich?"

"I don't know how I ate that one."

"When I get really angry I always get hungry. Luckily I rarely get angry."

"Thank God. I couldn't stand this very often."

"Then you're not going to wash your hands of me?"

"I love you. I'm just going to do my best to be on your side the next time.

Megan smiled. "What are we going to do? About Terry and Jeanette, I mean."

"I don't know," he said with a deep sigh.

"Do you want to back off? There's no reason for them to see me every time they see you."

"There is if we live together."

"Surely you can see we can't possibly do that. Not with them feeling this way."

"Megan, they're my daughters, and I love them dearly. But not like I love you. I won't give you up for anybody. Not even Terry and Jeanette."

"I can't live with you. I want to. I had almost decided to ask you to move in here, but I'm not going to. I can't do something that would put such a wedge between you and your children."

"Megan..."

"No."

He looked at her a long time before he nodded. "You're right. I just don't like it."

"Neither do I."

"Do you suppose it's this difficult for everybody who's trying to make a new life with someone?" Reid asked wistfully.

"I don't know. Maybe."

"We need to get away, to have some time to ourselves."

"What did you have in mind?"

"How about Florida?" he suggested.

"Sure. How about the moon, as well?"

"I'm serious. We could fly down, get some sun and soak up a little warmth before winter sets in. What do you think?"

"I've never been to Florida. Wait a minute—this isn't another trip down memory lane, is it?" Megan asked suspiciously.

"No way. Pamela gravitated toward California."

"Then let's go. I just needed to know the turf is all mine."

"It is. When can you leave?"

"Any time from half an hour on," Megan replied with a grin.

"I'll go in tomorrow morning and arrange everything from the office. Can you be ready for an afternoon flight?"

"I may not even need the plane."

He smiled at her and reached across the table for her hand. "I love you, Megan."

"I love you. Together we can lick this."

"I know we can."

She hoped they were right, but a part of her still had serious doubts.

Chapter Nine

The Florida sun felt warm and energizing to Megan as she and Reid followed the bellboy to their cabana. Beyond the small cottages the ocean rolled and purred beneath an endless sky. Gulls circled, their strident voices calling against the rustle of the palm trees in the breeze.

"It's hard to believe this is the same world," Megan said as Reid tipped the young man. "What a gorgeous place!"

The back wall of the sitting room in their cabana was mostly glass, affording a perfect view of the wide beach and blue-gray water. The room was decorated in shades of peach, silver and cream—beach colors. The same colors were repeated in the adjoining bedroom, and the splash of sunlight across the large bed told Megan that the outside wall in there must be glass as well.

"The travel agent said we'd be pleased with Vero Beach."

"It's not as crowded as I expected."

"This beach is owned by the hotel and reserved for hotel guests only. I'm sure the public beaches are solid humanity. Put on your suit, and let's go swimming."

She hurried to comply. "Who would have guessed I'd be swimming in October?" she marveled as she pulled up her one-piece swimsuit and fastened the straps behind her neck. "I had no intention of taking a vacation this year."

"I like your suit."

She turned to find Reid watching her, and she smiled almost shyly.

"Are you blushing?"

"I'm not used to dressing with someone else in the room, I guess. You're still so new to me." She watched as he shucked off his remaining clothes and pulled on a swimsuit. "I can get accustomed to it, however."

Reid traced his finger down one strap of her bright blue suit, over the mounds of her breasts and into the valley between. "Remind me to get you a bikini."

She laughed, feeling as if she were twenty again. "I'll race you to the beach."

He let her run ahead of him, then scooped her up and dashed into the waves with her shrieking in pretended fright. As a tall wave mounded in front of them, Reid turned his back to break the impact for Megan. Slowly he let her slide down his body until she stood beside him.

Seawater beaded on her skin and dewed her eyelashes as she flashed him a dazzling smile. "This is wonderful! I get so tired of cold weather."

"We'll come back often."

"Look out, here comes a big one!" The water buoyed her up as she spoke and sloshed her body against his.

"It was a friendly one," he said as he held her close to him. Another wave broke, sending sprays of salt water over them. He bent and kissed the salt from her lips as she clung to him, her feet floating off the ocean floor.

Together they splashed and romped like children in the water and on the sand. Exhausted, Megan flopped back on the warm beach and spread her arms wide. "This is great. Let's stay here forever."

"All right. As long as forever doesn't last past next Thursday. I have an important meeting then. You'll be glad to hear I've ordered changes in the catalytic heater. The meeting is to determine if the new model meets the While-Away standards."

"Good. Remind me to interview you again if it works." She closed her eyes and enjoyed the lazy warmth of the sun. When minutes passed and she heard nothing from Reid, she opened one eye. "What are you doing?"

"Building a sand condominium."

"You mean a castle," she said with a laugh.

"Nope. It has more potential as a condominium. Castles are passé."

Megan sat up and watched Reid square off the corners of his structure. He smoothed the top flat and began drawing the outline of a helicopter landing pad. Megan made a row of seashells for an outdoor terrace on the roof and made trees of seaweed.

Reid scooped away the sand at the base and carefully tunneled under the building. "Underground parking," he explained. His garage soon became too spacious, and the entire building collapsed.

"I guess that's why castles are better for sand sculpture," Megan said philosophically.

"Evidently."

She gazed at him, her eyes narrowed against the sun. "You aren't at all the way I thought you'd be. Whoever would have guessed Reid Spencer would be likely to play on a beach?''

"You expected me to swim in a tie and tails, perhaps?''

"Somehow I never pictured you at all out of an office.''

Reid lay back on the sand and said, "Before you came along, that was an accurate description of me. I worked late every night and rarely took a day off.''

"Why?''

"I think I was lonely.'' He took her hand and laced her fingers with his. "I had nothing at home, so I became engrossed in work.''

"You had Terry and Jeanette.''

"Daughters don't fill the kind of emptiness I had. It took you to do that.'' He thought for a minute and added, "I guess, too, I was afraid not to work. I saw Dad slave away day and night in that garage and heard Mom say she ached from being on her feet all day in the store. My job seemed so easy by comparison. I guess I thought if I didn't work hard at it that I might fail. I've always been afraid I'd be a failure.''

"You're the last person I'd suspect of that.''

"Now you know the secret to my drive. And if you print it, I'll wring your neck and deny every word.''

"Would I do a thing like that?''

"At one time you would have.''

Megan lay down beside him. "I guess you've changed me for the better, too.''

"Move in with me, and we'll both become perfect,'' he suggested only half playfully.

"No.''

"Marry me, then.''

Megan blinked. She couldn't possibly have heard him correctly. "What?"

"I asked you to marry me."

"Reid, I can't marry you. What would the children say?" She realized how ridiculous that sounded, and she laughed. "Besides, I don't think you're serious."

"There are two things no man in his right mind ever says unless he means them. One is 'I want a divorce,' and the other is 'Marry me.'"

She rolled to her side to face him. "You really mean it?"

He gazed steadily into her eyes. "You know I do."

"I have to think about it."

"What's there to think about? You love me, and I love you. We're certainly old enough to know our own minds."

"You know the idea of marriage frightens me."

"So, we'll tell everyone we're living in sin."

"Be serious."

"I am serious. I want you. It's taken me a while to decide I'm ready for a permanent commitment, but I know now that I am."

"But am I? Marriage isn't something to enter into lightly."

"You think these past few days have been all sweetness and light? If so, I think your memory has gone haywire."

She drew her finger across the sand that dusted his chest. "What if I marry you and you die or something?"

"What if you don't marry me and I die or something? Will I be any less gone? Megan, we have years and years left. I want to spend them all with you."

"Your daughters will have fits."

"They already have."

"What if this drives a wedge between you and them forever? No, I can't take that chance."

"You'd rather they came between us?"

"No one can do that. I love you, and I've told you I don't fall in love casually."

"Then your answer is no?"

"I want to try to win them over first."

"Then your answer is yes?"

"My answer is a definite maybe."

He sighed. "When will you decide?"

"Let me try to get into their good graces, especially after that scene last night. If we go back and announce we're getting married, they may never speak to us again."

"Honey, you don't know them like I do. Terry is full of dramatics, and Jeanette follows her lead in everything. They put on quite a performance, but I don't believe they really meant it."

"No?"

"They love me. Naturally they want me to be happy. After you left I told them you are the key to my happiness and that they will simply have to accept it."

"And?"

"I'm beginning to wonder if Pamela is behind their actions."

"I wouldn't be a bit surprised. She came to see me the other day."

"She did? Pamela? Why?"

"To tell me to quit seeing you. She said that without me in the picture, you would go back to her."

"That's out of the question!"

"Exactly what I told her. She's a pretty fair dramatic actress herself."

"I wish you had told me. I'll see to it that she doesn't do it again."

"No need for you to do that. I can take care of myself. That's why I saw no reason to tell you."

"Then she probably *is* the reason the girls are so upset about you. Of course! I should have seen it all along." He sat up and wrapped his arms around his knees. "This simplifies everything. I didn't think Terry and Jeanette were that selfish. All I have to do is make it clear to them that I'm not coming back to their mother."

"How do you propose to do that?"

"I'll just explain it to them. They're almost adults. They'll understand."

"Right." She couldn't sound convinced. All she could see was Terry throwing a tantrum and Jeanette crying as if the world were ending. Surely all that wasn't a result of Pamela's desire to sabotage Megan's relationship with Reid.

"Don't you feel, right this minute, as if you could win any battle? I do. Being with you makes me feel like that."

Megan smiled. "You affect me the same way. Maybe I am building this up out of proportion about the girls. After all, you know them better than I do."

"That's right. Together we can overcome anything."

"I love you, Reid. I love your optimism and your enthusiasm and the way you tilt at windmills."

"The other secret to my success is my single-mindedness. Once I make up my mind to do something, I do it."

"Like marrying me?"

"Absolutely. And I'll have the girls eating out of your hand in no time."

"I'm not entirely sure I want to hand-feed them. They might bite," she observed wryly.

"The only one likely to bite you is me." He grinned as he leaned toward her. "But I guarantee you won't mind."

"Promise?" Her eyes were teasing as she touched her nose to his.

"Let's go inside, and I'll prove it. Besides, you don't want to get a sunburn. Not with an entire week to play in the sun."

Megan let him pull her to her feet, and hand in hand they went back to the cabana.

"I like being here with you," she said as he closed the door to shut out the world.

"Come here, you sexy devil," he growled as he pulled her into his embrace.

She kissed his shoulder and wrinkled her nose. "Sand!"

In the bathroom they undressed each other as the Roman tub, complete with whirlpool, was filling. Megan eased in and slid low in the hot water. "This is positively decadent," she sighed as Reid turned on the whirlpool action and stepped in.

A seashell-shaped dish held pink perfumed soap, and Reid smoothed it over her body, then rinsed away the foam. "I love the way your skin feels when it's wet. You're so soft and smooth."

She turned so that she lay back against him and leaned her head on his shoulder. Reid cupped her breasts in his hands and rubbed his thumbs lightly over her nipples. Megan closed her eyes and let him give her pleasure as she all but purred in satisfaction.

"Do you like this?" he asked.

"I love it."

"How about this?" He slid one hand down her slick skin to gently nudge her legs apart.

Megan murmured happily as he gently stroked the bud of her pleasure. His fingers were all-knowing as he brought her greater and greater pleasure. Suddenly she cried out as he strummed her to an unexpected completion. Megan felt as if all her bones had gone soft, and she floated in Reid's arms.

Again his fingers began to spin their magic, and she turned to face him as her passion reawakened. In one fluid movement she took him into her warmth and entwined her arms around his neck. Sensuously she moved, setting the pace, giving him pleasure as he had given it to her. Her body responded as she sensed his passion building. When neither could stand to prolong the fervor any longer, Megan shifted to bring him deeper within her, and they soared together in their shared culmination.

"You're wonderful," he whispered a few moments later as he held her close. "Marry me."

"That's not fair. I can't say no to you at a time like this."

"Then you will marry me?"

"No. You don't play fair."

"You're the most exasperating woman I've ever met." She kissed him and gazed into his eyes. "Possibly."

"I won't give up, you know."

"I just don't want to rush into something. Look how fast all this has happened."

He pulled her head down to his shoulder. "We'll work it out, darling. We love each other too much not to."

She nodded against the wet satin of his skin.

During the days they walked on the beach or enjoyed the ocean waves. At night they made love in the wide bed with the ocean serenading them with its ceaseless, primal rhythm.

"I wish we could stay here forever," Megan said as Reid zipped up her navy blouson dress. She smoothed the pleated skirt and fastened the pearl buttons on the cuffs of her chiffon sleeves.

"Being here with you has been wonderful," he agreed as he dropped a light kiss on her neck. "Waking up with you, holding you while we sleep. Having you within my reach day and night."

"I almost dread going back."

"We can come again."

She turned and put her arms around his neck. "I love you, Reid."

"You're my special lady." He kissed her gently and enjoyed the sensation of her body pressed close to his. "Maybe I should cancel our dinner reservations."

"You're insatiable," she said with a laugh. "And I love it."

"I bought you something." He reached into his coat pocket and brought out a small jeweler's box.

"When did you have time to go shopping?"

"I went out this afternoon while you were taking a nap."

She opened the box and exclaimed with delight when she saw the golden heart. "It's beautiful!"

"I thought you'd like it. When I saw it in the store I knew it would be perfect for you."

"But, Reid, it must have been very expensive!"

"I'm not a poor man, darling. This is one of the advantages of success." He fastened the thin golden chain around her neck and surveyed her in the mirror. "Lovely!"

"Thank you. I'll always treasure it."

"And me?"

"I treasure you much, much more."

They left the cabana and strolled over the carefully manicured green to the hotel lobby. A waiting cab took them to an address a few blocks down the coast.

"How pretty! You made a good selection."

"I told the hotel manager I wanted the perfect place, since this is our last night here. I must admit, this is even better than I expected."

To enter the thatched building, they passed through an avenue of tall palms. A waterfall splashed loudly outside the front door, and inside, the motif was Polynesian. On the far wall another waterfall careened down rocks into a stream that branched among the tables, dividing the restaurant into a series of islands. Arched bridges provided paths from one island to the next.

"It's like a fantasy world," Megan said as they followed the waiter past a grouping of native totem poles half-hidden by live bamboo fronds.

Reid held the wicker chair for her and sat opposite. "I want tonight to be perfect."

"It already is."

"You've shown me so much. I've never seen anyone so alive as you. Without you I never would have tasted medieval food or met mountaineers who make dulcimers and wall hangings. You've opened up new vistas for me."

"I'm just being me. You've been a good influence on me, as well. I've always lived rather hand-to-mouth, and if I ran out of money I just made do until I could sell another article. I've never paid much attention to the idea that I might need more stability. You've been a steadying influence. Together we make quite a team."

"That's what I've been trying to tell you."

They gave the sarong-clad waitress their order, and when she left Reid said, "Do you regret not taking the assignment in Africa?"

"Not at all. It's funny, isn't it? I would have sworn that I would jump at an opportunity like that, but I felt no letdown at all when I refused it. I told you that you had made me more stable."

"I hope I haven't clipped your wings. I want you to be free."

"I am," she said with a happy sigh. "I've never felt so free before in my entire life. Whoever would have guessed that love could do that? I mean, you'd think I'd feel the weight of responsibility again. Instead I feel as if I can do anything, be anything, with you beside me."

"Good. You had me worried for a minute there. After all, I'm stable enough for both of us."

"Not as much of a type-A, however. I'll bet you haven't thought of work for days."

"At least not very often," he conceded. "I enjoy my work."

"I like mine, too. I have an idea for a series of articles on the southwestern Indians. I want to use the angle of a woman's role in the tribe, both in the past and in the present."

"Sounds interesting."

"When I get home I'll query some magazines. I know a family that lives just west of Denver near Idaho Springs. I think I'll start my interviews with them."

"Have you ever considered writing a book?"

"Yes, but I've never had time. The articles bring in a comfortable living but not enough padding to take the time I'd need for an entire book."

"I could be your patron."

"A book," she said thoughtfully. "I've always wanted to write one. Not much is written on some of the Indian tribes. I have good sources of information."

"I think you should try it."

She shook her head. "I can't let you support me while I write. I don't like what that would make me."

"I had in mind that it would make you my wife."

"Reid, I want to marry you. I want it more than anything. But I couldn't bear it if our marriage drove away your daughters."

"I keep trying to tell you that I know them better than that. True, they behaved badly the other night, but they weren't expecting it. Now they've had time to get used to the idea that we're in love. Kids are basically selfish—it's just part of being a child. Terry and Jeanette are almost grown, however, and I know they'll come around."

"Still, we shouldn't spring too much on them too fast."

"Does it make sense for two adults to be ruled by two teenagers? Come on now, Megan."

"No, that isn't right, either, but your relationship with them is important."

Their food was served, and Megan was thoughtful as she ate. His daughters aside, life with Reid would be exciting and at the same time comfortable. They enjoyed doing the same things, and their thinking seemed to run on the same track. Often he voiced her thoughts and vice versa. She no longer had qualms about keeping him from Pamela, for she knew that was all finished. The only stumbling block was his daughters.

After they finished eating, Reid led her to the small dance floor at the rear of the restaurant, where they glided into the easy rhythm of a popular song.

"You dance as perfectly as you do everything else," she said. "Is there anything you don't do well?"

"I'm not good at talking you into things."

"I'm afraid we're both pretty stubborn. Can you get used to it?"

"I'm learning to."

As the music wafted around them, Megan floated in Reid's arms. He was a superb dancer and led her into complicated turns that seemed effortless. "I've never danced with anyone like you."

"It's becoming a lost art, I'm afraid. Teenagers either aren't touching at all or they're draped over each other and barely moving."

"That's exactly what my parents said about me when I was a teenager," she said with a laugh. "I guess it all comes full circle."

"Maybe our grandchildren will bring back ballroom dancing."

"Our grandchildren," she mused. "I hadn't thought of that."

"You really wish you had children, don't you? I can see it in your eyes."

"It's my only real disappointment. But first Hugh wanted to wait; then we found out how sick he was. He didn't want to leave me with the extra burden of children to raise alone. I wish I could have changed his mind, but I couldn't." After a moment she said, "Do you really think Terry and Jeanette will learn to accept me?"

"They'll have to. You're far too important for me to give you up."

"That's how I feel, too. Every day I love you more."

The music ended, and they threaded their way back to their table. Megan said, "Are you ready to leave? I thought perhaps we could walk back along the beach."

"Sure." He paid the waitress, and they went out into the balmy night.

The wind off the ocean was fresh with the scent of salt, and above them arched countless stars. A waxing moon gave them enough light to see, and when they reached the end of the boardwalk to the beach, they paused so she could remove her heels before stepping into the sand.

Reid slipped one shoe into each of his coat pockets and took her hand. "I'm glad you thought of this. A moonlight stroll along the beach is the ideal way to end the evening."

The ocean mumbled against the pewter shore, and silver froth limned the inky waves. Megan drew in a deep breath and said, "Just smell the air! I never knew how much I'd love the beach."

"Surely you've been to the ocean before."

"Yes, but not since I was a girl. It's much more fun without my mother calling out for me not to do things. She's such a worrier."

"I'll bet you were a handful," he teased her with a chuckle. "She probably had cause to worry."

Megan laughed. "That could be."

They walked in silence for a while, then Megan said, "I've been thinking. Let's get married."

Reid stopped in his tracks. "What?"

"All that you've said makes sense. Why shouldn't two people marry when they're this much in love? Jeanette and Terry will be a problem, but I can win them over in time. If we're married, they're much more likely to accept me than they will if I'm just your friend."

"Megan." Reid drew her to him.

The moonlight made his hair as silver as the breaking waves, and although she couldn't see his eyes, she heard the vast relief in his voice. "Megan, my Megan."

"I love you," she whispered.

"God, I love you." He claimed her lips with all the passion in his heart. When he drew back, his voice was shaky. "I was so afraid you'd never agree to marry me."

"I had to be sure. It's going to last forever, you know. You don't have to worry about that."

"I know. I can feel it. You're the one I was meant to find. Together we make two halves of a whole."

"Soul mates?" she asked with a smile. "I feel it, too. I suspect we couldn't give each other up if we tried."

"Let's never try."

"From now on things will be easier. With so much love between us, how can they be otherwise?"

"You're right. As for the girls, well, they've missed having two parents under the same roof. You'll make a wonderful mother for them."

Megan's smile broadened. "Me, a mother! I like that. We'll show them how a marriage should be. Children learn best by example. They'll see how happy we are, and they'll be happy, too."

"I love you, Megan. I still can hardly believe it. When do you want the wedding to be?"

"How about the first part of November? That gives us almost a month to arrange things and for the girls to get accustomed to the idea."

"That'll be more than enough time." He kissed her again, savoring the sweetness of her mouth and the warmth of her breath upon his cheek. "What about a honeymoon?"

"I have a feeling the rest of our lives will be one."

"Just the same, I want to take you somewhere special. How about Europe?"

"Europe! You mean the one over the ocean? That Europe?"

"Would you like that?"

"I never dreamed of seeing Europe! Can we really do something like that? I mean, you just took off this past week."

"That's one of the advantages of being president of my own company."

"It would be terribly expensive."

"That's another advantage."

Megan laughed with sheer delight. "I'd love to go to Europe. Reid, could we see a castle?"

"Dozens of them. Would you like to stay in one?"

"A castle! Think of what I could write when we came home!" She sighed ecstatically but said practically, "Let's wait until spring. That way we'll see the wildflowers and not just snow."

"All right. Whatever you want. I'm going to spend the rest of my life making you happy."

"Just be with me. The happiness will be automatic. I love you so. You don't think I'm marrying you for your money, do you?"

He threw back his head and laughed. "If you were, I wouldn't have spent the entire week trying to convince you to marry me! No, darling, I'd never think that."

"Your friends might."

"No, my friends won't. Besides, I don't care what anyone else thinks."

Megan looped her arm around his waist as they resumed their walk back to the hotel. "I'm going to love being your wife."

"I guess I should move into your house. As you've pointed out, all our things would never fit into my apartment. Or maybe we should buy a new house."

"Not yet. I've always loved that house. It's like an old friend."

"Then we'll keep it. We're going to be very happy together."

"Megan Spencer. I like the sound of it."

"So do I. Are you really determined to wait a month?" Reid asked.

"Yes. I think that will be easier for your daughters."

"You're going to make a good mother."

"Before we leave tomorrow I want to go shopping. I want to bring them each a gift. I was thinking about it earlier, and I know just what to get them."

Reid smiled down at her. She was so wonderful. How could she think the girls wouldn't love her?

Chapter Ten

Quit looking so nervous. This isn't the inquisition."

"No, but it never occurred to me that they would know we went away together."

"What difference does it make? We don't have to have their permission."

"Don't you see, Reid? I'm trying to impress them favorably."

"Just because Pamela knows doesn't mean the girls do."

"Why did you tell her?"

"I didn't volunteer it. She asked if you went with me to Florida, and I said yes. Quit pacing."

Megan looked out the window. "They're here. So is Pamela."

The girls walked slowly into the house, and Megan saw at once that they knew about the vacation to Florida.

Pamela put an arm around each girl and gave Reid a martyred look. "Hello, Reid."

"Hello," he said abruptly. To the girls he said, "Hi, Terry, Jeanette. Are you ready for a terrific weekend?"

"I guess," Terry mumbled. Jeanette simply nodded.

"Aren't you feeling well?" He put his hand on Jeanette's forehead.

"They know you went away with...her...to Florida," Pamela stated.

"I brought you girls something," Megan said brightly as she reached for the two gifts.

Pamela pretended not to hear her. "Reid, I'm so disappointed in you. This has upset them very much."

"Then why did you tell them?" he countered. "Come on in, girls, and have some brownies."

"Who made them?" Terry asked.

"I did," Megan admitted.

"No, thanks. I'm on a diet."

"Brownies?" Jeanette said with interest.

"She shouldn't have any. She has to learn to watch her weight now that she's growing up," Pamela said, watching Megan.

"I think Jeanette is lovely just as she is," Megan said as she held out the plate of brownies to Jeanette.

"No, thanks," Jeanette said reluctantly.

"Reid, could I talk to you alone?"

"No, Pamela, you can't. Anything you have to say to me you can say in front of Megan."

Pamela's big gray eyes began to fill with tears. "No, there are some things I can't. Not without making a fool of myself."

"Reid, it's all right," Megan said quickly. "It will give me a chance to talk to the girls."

Reluctantly Reid followed Pamela out to the doorstep and shut the door behind him.

"Is it true you and my dad went on a trip together?" Jeanette asked.

Megan swallowed. "Yes, we did."

"Why?"

"Because we're in love and we want to be together." She again picked up the two gifts. "Here. I brought you these."

"We're not babies," Terry said scornfully.

"I know. I did it because I wanted to give you something."

With an audible sigh, Terry pulled the paper from her gift. "A book on acting?"

"I know you want to be an actress."

"Actresses are born, not made by reading a book." She tossed it onto the couch.

Megan bit back her retort. She wouldn't gain anything by upbraiding the girl.

Jeanette tore through the wrapping paper, opened the box and appreciatively held up a coral necklace. "Oh," she murmured. "It's so pretty!"

With relief Megan smiled. At least one gift had been right. "When I saw it I thought of you. Would you like me to put it on you?"

Jeanette nodded and held her dark hair out of the way. Megan felt a surprising flow of maternal love as her fingers brushed the girl's neck. This would soon be her daughter. "It looks very nice on you."

"Is it plastic?" Terry asked.

"It's pink coral," Megan said.

Terry shrugged. "I think it looks like plastic."

Reid came in, his face taut. Megan smiled brittlely and clasped her cold hands in front of her. "See how nice the necklace looks on Jeanette?"

"Very nice," Reid said with a forced smile. "Terry, did you open your gift?"

"It's a book."

Reid opened the book and glanced through it as if he found it fascinating. "There's some good stuff in here."

"Oh, Dad," Terry groaned.

Jeanette fingered the necklace thoughtfully. "Why did you bring us gifts?"

Reid met Megan's eyes and said, "Megan was thinking of you. She picked out things she thought you'd enjoy." He put his hands into the pockets of his tan cords and studied his daughters. "I just told your mother something that I had intended to tell you first." He pushed up the sleeves of his teal and navy rugby sweater and sat between them on the couch. "I know how much you've missed having two parents together. Well, I'm going to change that."

"What!" Terry's face brightened, and she threw herself into Reid's arms as Jeanette squealed happily. "When?"

"At the beginning of next month." He cuddled his daughters and grinned at Megan over the tops of their heads. "I knew you'd be pleased."

"Pleased? I'm ecstatic!" Terry gushed.

"Me, too!" Jeanette said as she hugged him tightly. "When will you be home exactly?"

Megan was instantly paralyzed as her brain flashed a red warning signal of the pending disaster. She opened her mouth to protest, but nothing came out at first. On the second try she heard herself almost shouting, "You don't understand. He means he's marrying me."

Terry and Jeanette both exclaimed. "You!"

"That's right. I'm going to be your stepmother. But I hope we'll be as close as mother and daughters."

"Gross!" Terry exploded. "We don't want you!"

Jeanette looked from one to the other as her eyes filled with tears.

"Jeanette, don't cry," Megan said as she put her arms around the younger girl. "I know you're a little surprised, but—"

"That's not the word for it!" Jeanette jerked away savagely. "No wonder you bought us these things! You were trying to bribe us!"

"I wasn't!"

"I can't believe you're doing this!" Terry ground out. "Did you really think we would be happy?"

"Girls, calm down!" Reid said sharply. "I've had enough of this. We told you last week that we love each other. You must have at least considered that we might marry."

"No!" Jeanette sniffed. "Mom always said you'd come back to us in time."

"Jeanette, she left me, not the other way around. You know that. I've told you time and again that that marriage is finished."

"Why would you want to marry her?" Terry spat out. "Mom is younger and prettier!"

"Terry!"

Megan's eyes blazed with anger, and she barely managed to control her temper. "Your father and I love each other, and we're going to be married the first weekend of November. We would like you two to be our attendants."

"Me? Be in your wedding?" Terry sputtered. "Never!"

"What's an attendant?" Jeanette asked as she wiped her eyes."

"It's like a maid of honor. You'll wear a pretty dress and stand at the altar beside us," Megan said in a gentler voice. "Would you like that?"

"Jeanette!" Terry said warningly.

Jeanette jumped. "No. I want Dad to marry Mom again."

"See? She doesn't want you, either!"

Megan clasped the gold heart Reid had given her and tried to feel his reassurance through it as he scolded both girls roundly. How could she live with such constant animosity? She thought Jeanette might come around in time without Terry's interference, but she saw no hope of peace between Terry and herself. And Terry obviously controlled Jeanette pretty thoroughly. Megan let the locket drop back to her dark green sweater and tried again. "I know you're upset, but try to see it our way. If you were grown up and in love, wouldn't you want to be together?"

"Dad loved Mom. Why do you think he'll stay with you?"

"Terry, if you keep it up, I'm taking you home," Reid threatened.

Terry leaned against his side and glared at Megan. "You're making a mistake, Dad. I don't want you to be unhappy."

"Being married to Megan will make me very happy."

"There's not much room here for someone else," Jeanette said as she clung to his other side. "Where will we put her things?"

"I'm going to move to her place. You'll love it. It's an old Victorian house with fancy trim and a porch swing."

"I won't love it," Jeanette affirmed.

Megan knelt in front of Reid to place a hand on the knee of each girl. "I know you're afraid of the changes that are happening, but you shouldn't be. Your father and I want you to be happy. You can come and go over there just as you do here. The only difference is that we'll be married."

"That's some difference!" Terry said. "Dad, what about the tennis courts and the swimming pool here? We won't have any place to play or swim."

"Maybe we could put in a pool," he suggested. At Megan's nod he added, "An indoor one that we can use all year."

"An indoor pool?" Jeanette's voice held a spark of interest.

"We can all play tennis at the public courts," Megan said. "It'll be fun."

Jeanette smiled tremulously, but Terry continued to scowl as she said, "You can't buy my affection with a dumb old pool."

"We weren't trying to buy your affections," Reid said. "Come on now. Act right."

After a long look full of animosity aimed at Megan, Terry put her arms around Reid's neck. "I'm sorry, Dad."

"Me, too. And I really do like my necklace." Jeanette hugged him tightly.

Megan watched them, and when Reid smiled at her, she managed to smile back. She knew the battle had just begun in winning the girls' affection. Terry surreptitiously moved her leg so that Megan was no longer touching her. Megan felt very lonely as she watched Reid hug his daughters and tell them again how happy they would all be. She was afraid she would always be an outsider to them.

For the rest of the evening Megan wondered about the likelihood of the girls learning to care for her. At the moment she would settle for even mild friendliness. Whenever she thought of her future with Reid, she experienced a curious emotional split. On one hand she loved him and knew he loved her. She was sure the marriage would be a good one. But on the other hand, she was still very fearful of losing him. She knew for a fact that simply loving someone was no assurance of not being parted from him.

"You seem to be very deep in thought," Reid observed as they were returning from taking the girls home.

"Yes, I was thinking."

"You're not changing your mind, are you?"

"No, no, of course not."

"I think the girls are beginning to come around, don't you? They were even laughing by the time we dropped them off."

"They were laughing with you. Neither of them spoke to me at all."

"I think you're imagining things. I didn't notice them ignoring you."

Megan made no comment. She knew it wasn't her imagination. "Tomorrow I'll call the church and make arrangements for the ceremony."

"Great. I'll call the travel agency and have them start looking for something special this spring. Are you sure you want to delay our honeymoon?"

"I heard Terry telling Jeanette that we'd already had our honeymoon."

"I didn't hear that."

"You were in the kitchen at the time."

"Terry says she thinks she'll get a scholarship to Colorado State through the drama department."

Megan made the proper responses, but her mind was far away. The few times she had considered remarriage she had assumed it would be as simple as her first wedding. In her wildest dreams she had never thought two consenting adults would encounter such conflict over getting married. Megan didn't know exactly what Pamela might do, but she fully expected her to cause trouble. Megan was certain Pamela was contributing to the problem with the girls. Nothing else seemed reasonable. As Reid said, Terry and Jeanette were nearly adults. His remarrying after being divorced for two years was scarcely a big shock, particularly since their mother had already done it.

She asked Reid inside when they reached her house, but she still couldn't shake her sense of foreboding. The more she loved Reid, the more she had to lose. He built a fire in the fireplace and motioned for her to sit beside him on the couch. Megan curled against his side and rested her head on his shoulder as she watched the flames lick at the logs.

Rather wistfully Reid said, "I was having a fantasy while I watched you and the girls tonight. I was wondering what it would be like if they lived with us."

Megan's eyes flew open. "Do you think they might?"

"No, I guess there's no chance. Their mother would never give them up. Besides, Terry graduates this coming spring and will be going away to college."

"That still leaves Jeanette."

"Pamela is Super Mom. She couldn't bear the idea of either girl living away from her until the last possible moment."

"I have to admit, the idea seems pretty scary to me."

"If you and the girls saw each other every day and were living under the same roof, you'd soon become close. I've seen it happen with my friends and their stepchildren."

"For a while, at least, I hope I'll have you all to myself. Is that selfish?"

"Yes, and I love it. I want you all to myself, too. I wasn't suggesting we try to move the girls in with us. It was just an idle fantasy." He rubbed his cheek on her hair. "You're being unusually quiet. Are you sure nothing is wrong?"

"Not really. I'm still just trying to get used to the idea of being married again."

"We're going to be very happy. Love like this doesn't come along very often."

"I know. That's part of what scares me. Isn't that silly? I'm worried because I'm so happy. It reminds me of my Irish grandmother saying not to be too happy or the angels will get jealous." Her voice faltered.

"I have it on good authority that angels don't do that."

She laughed. "I said it was silly."

"I guess in thirty or forty years you'll believe me." He tilted her face up to his and kissed her gently. "I love you, lady. Silly ideas and all."

"Oh, yeah? You won't mind an occasional medieval meal or traipsing over mountains with me? It won't bother you that my house always seems to be cluttered with my most recent research?"

"I'm looking forward to it—all of it."

Megan reached up to stroke his handsome face and thread her fingers through his enchanting silver hair. Her eyes were shiny with love, and he smiled as he studied her features. "You know, I'm glad we met now instead of earlier," he said.

"I was just wishing I had known you all my life."

"Now is better. My finances are secure, and I know we'll never have to scrimp and save to make ends meet. I wish we could have raised a family together, but now we both know who we are and exactly what we want out of life. We missed the first blush of youth, but we're also past the insecurities and giddiness."

"Speak for yourself," Megan retorted. "I've been told I'll never grow up."

"Not by me, you haven't. If you mean by not growing up that you'll never believe in the negative more than the positive or that you'll be forever chasing rainbows and looking for fairies, then I agree. And I wouldn't have you any other way."

"I sometimes go off on wild tangents," she cautioned him with a smile. "I'd pan for gold in ditch water if I saw something shiny. I've been known to adopt rabbits with broken legs and whole litters of kittens. You just happened to catch me between pets."

"I like animals. I can also learn to pan for gold in ditches. Who knows? We might find some."

Megan looked deep into his eyes and saw the man she had been created to match. She felt as if they had loved forever, yet the excitement was fresh and alive. "When you look at me like that I smell orange blossoms and believe in happily ever after."

"That's good, because that's the way it's going to be." He bent his head and kissed her, a gentle and lingering kiss that deepened as her lips parted under his.

His tongue traced the moist recesses of her mouth, and Megan returned his kiss with growing passion. He slipped a hand beneath the thick knit of her sweater to cup her breast. Megan sighed and closed her eyes as he caressed the lacy wisp of her bra, teasing her tightening nipple.

"Come to bed with me," she whispered. "I want to make love with you."

He smiled and paused only long enough to close the glass fire doors on the hearth before following her up the stairs.

When Megan awoke, Reid was gone, and she rolled to his side of the bed. Dawn was sending a pearl-rose glow through the window to chase away the night shadows. She pulled the lace bedspread up under her chin and looked objectively at her room. Years before she had papered it in a decidedly frilly pattern, and her bedspread was made of eyelet edged with deep flounces of lace. This was not a room suitable to share with a man, she concluded. As the daylight brightened, she decided to buy new wallpaper that would reflect the tastes of both Reid and herself. She could move the lace bedspread to one of the two guest rooms. She expected it would suit Jeanette more than Terry. The past was over, and she was ready for the future.

Feeling a burst of energy, Megan jumped out of bed and showered as she planned her day. Reid's suggestion that she write a book had given her a lot to consider. Very few books had been written on local native people, probably because even now the tribes tended to be closed to outsiders and not free with information. She, however, was friends with a number of natives, and she felt they would trust her to write accurately about their customs.

As she dressed she began to mentally outline the chapters she would include. She wanted the book to focus on the lives of native women. Almost everything written was about the men as warriors and their battles with the whites. Megan wanted to show the hopes and strengths of the women who lived mostly in the shadows of history.

Her thoughts were racing as she threw some clothes into a zippered bag. This could be a book that might receive national acclaim. This could mean far more to her career than the trip to Africa, or even *National Geographic*.

She dialed Reid's number, but the phone rang without answer. A glance at her watch told her the office switchboard wasn't open yet. With a shrug, she shouldered her bag. She could call him tonight from Idaho Springs and tell him where she had gone. In an hour she was past Denver and heading west on I-70 toward the home of a family of White River Utes who lived in the mountains.

Joseph Antelope and his wife, Sarah, were in the field near the small house when Megan arrived. She waved and let herself into the field through the wooden gate. At once a pack of tail-wagging dogs surrounded her. The dogs were of every color and no particular breed, and all acted as glad to see Megan as the swarm of copper-hued children that followed them. Megan greeted the children by name and went out to join Sarah and Joseph.

"Your children are growing so fast! Tony is taller than I am, and his voice is changing." She lifted the youngest of the brood and said, "I brought you all some cookies, Maria. Give me a hug and ask Tony to look in a bag in the front seat of my car." She put the girl down and held out her hand to Joseph.

"Welcome, Megan. We haven't seen you in a long time. I'm surprised you have come this late in the year."

"You'll stay with us," Sarah said decisively. "Your room is always ready."

"No, thanks, Sarah. This trip I have to stay in town. I've already checked into a motel in Idaho Springs."

"Such a drive!"

"I know, but I need to type, and it will keep the little ones awake." She knew this was true, because "her" room was one she shared with the younger girls.

"I was hoping this was a visit and not work. What are you writing?" Joseph asked.

"I have a marvelous idea. I'm going to do a book about several Indian tribes from the women's perspective. I want to interview your grandmother."

Joseph smiled. "She'll love it. She always talks your ear off anyway. Come inside. She will have heard the car and is probably wondering who came. We don't get many visitors, you know."

"If you'd put in a phone, I could have called. I hope I'm not interrupting anything."

"How can a friend interrupt? I guess I'll put in a phone someday, but my friends' phones seem to ring all the time. We wouldn't have a peaceful moment."

"Tony would love one," Sarah said. "I have a feeling our peace is short-lived. The children are growing up, and they want contact with their friends."

They let Megan precede them into the compact house, and she smiled when she noticed that the children were devouring the cookies, and sharing them with their incredibly old grandmother. Juanita Antelope looked like a dried-apple doll wrapped in a bright blanket. Her seamed face brightened when she saw Megan, and her first words were, "What are you doing out here? You should be in town looking for a husband."

Megan laughed and sat on a footstool beside the old woman. "There's no need to, Grannie Juanita. I've found one."

"What?" Sarah exclaimed. "You never told us!"

"It's a rather new development. We're getting married next month."

The old woman grinned, showing toothless gums. "A winter bride. Good! Very lucky."

"How's that lucky, Grannie?" Joseph asked. "I never heard that."

"The baby will come in the summer. His feet won't be cold."

"I doubt there will be a baby," Megan said with a smile. "Reid already has two daughters, both a little older than Tony."

"Only two? He's barely begun." Juanita waved her paper-thin hand in dismissal, and her black eyes twinkled.

"I've come especially to see you this trip, Grannie Juanita. I'm writing a book, and I want to ask you about your grandmother."

Juanita smiled as Megan turned on her tape recorder and nodded for her to begin. "She was named Bird Song, and she knew the great Chief Ouray and his wife, Chipeta. My grandmother spoke very little English. We have been Ute for as long as there have been people. Her father was Topanas, and her son was named Ku-ri-en. He was my father."

"What were a woman's duties in Bird Song's time?"

With a laugh, Juanita said, "Women were responsible for almost everything except hunting and fishing and making war."

"Did they grow crops?"

"No. Utes were not farmers. Not in our days of greatness. We were hunters and warriors. Everyone feared the people."

"Tell Megan about weaving," Sarah prompted.

"Not much to tell. We made everything but fish traps. Men made those. We soaked willow strips in a pond to limber them up, then wove them into jugs or bowls. Afterward we coated them with clay and baked them in the sun." She shrugged. "How else would they be made? We also wove sleeping mats of willow."

"The Utes in Utah made a kind of flax from the stems of dog bane and stinging nettle," Sarah added.

"It could only be made in autumn," the old woman said with a nod. "Before that the plants were too green, and afterward their strength dried up."

"So you've done these things yourself?"

Juanita laughed softly. "Many times. Many times. When I was a girl we didn't live so easy a life as my grandson does."

Megan knew Sarah and Joseph Antelope worked hard and were far from rich, but as Juanita continued, Megan saw that their life was indeed easier.

"We ate sap from willow trees. It was taken by cutting the bark and letting the sap run out through a hollow bone or a reed. That way the tree wasn't killed. Nuts from piñon pinecones were one of our main foods. Cloth or hides were spread on the ground, then women beat the trees with long sticks. After the nuts were gathered, they were put in large willow trays along with hot rocks. The rocks and nuts had to be tossed without stopping or the rocks would burn holes in the tray. After a while the nuts were roasted and could be shelled and eaten or ground into meal. To cook the meal, it was dampened into balls and boiled or baked on hot rocks. Baked was best, I think."

Although the recorder was still taping, Megan was busy jotting down notes on the old woman's expressions and gesticulations. Later she would incorporate every detail into her writing.

Sarah went into the kitchen and returned with a handful of tiny nuts. "Here are some if you want to try them."

"You still bake them?"

Juanita gave forth her velvety laugh again as Sarah said, "Of course."

The nuts were sweet and oily, and the flavor was remarkably good. Megan made notes hastily as Juanita moved into reminiscences of stories the women told as they gathered their family's food or were confined to the brush shelters during their "time of womanhood," as Juanita delicately termed it.

The old woman had a wealth of information, and before she was finished Megan had several tapes and pages of notes. The sky outside the window was black. Regretfully Megan stood and straightened her cramped muscles. Except for a brief lunch break, she had sat there all day.

"You aren't leaving," Juanita protested as Megan put on her coat. "You can't go in the dark."

"I must. I've already checked into the motel in town."

"I may remember more tales after supper."

"I'll be back. I don't want to tire you."

"How can I be tired from remembering?" But Megan saw that the old woman was in need of rest.

She patted the thin hand and said, "I'll come back again soon. Next time we'll talk about your grandchildren."

Juanita smiled at the blue-black heads of the children playing on the floor. "They are good babies. But you must bring your man when you come. I have to see him. See if he will take proper care of you."

"Grannie!" Joseph protested.

"I'll bring him."

"Joseph, go to my room and get the box where I keep things."

When Joseph returned with a box woven of pine needles dyed red and blue, Juanita nodded in satisfaction. Opening the lid, she poked through until she found a necklace made of colored beads and quills with a skillfully executed medallion. "Wear this on your wedding day."

"How beautiful!" Megan exclaimed. "I couldn't possibly accept it."

"You have no grandmother of your own to make you pretty things. It is yours."

"Thank you. I'll think of you when I wear it. It's a lovely wedding gift."

Juanita snorted. "A man makes bridal gifts to his wife. This is a love gift. Have you heard nothing I've said? I give this to you because you drive many miles and sit long hours on an uncomfortable stool to listen to an old Indian woman talk about days that will never come again."

Megan hugged Juanita and smiled. "I never grow tired of hearing you, Grannie Juanita. Next time I come, I'll bring Reid."

"Reed. It is a good name. Reeds bend but don't break, and their heads always point up at the sky toward Sineuwa, the creator. One of my uncles was named Reed-in-Water."

Sarah and Joseph walked out to the car with Megan. Because the night was crisp, Joseph put his arm around his wife to keep her warm.

"I hope I didn't exhaust her. I didn't realize how long we talked until I saw how dark it was."

"She loved it. She misses her friends. Most of them are dead now, or bedridden."

Megan held out the necklace to Sarah. "I really shouldn't keep this. Your own daughters should wear it at their weddings."

Sarah closed Megan's hand over the necklace. "Grannie Juanita made it in her youth, and it's hers to give away. We would be shamed if we took it back."

Megan hesitated, then released the clasp of the opal pendant she wore. "Will you accept this in return? It's one I've loved and worn often. It will look very pretty on your daughters."

Sarah's smile was instantaneous. "I am honored. It will be handed down from bride to bride as my grandmother's necklace was."

"And I will see to it that this one is also kept in my family," Megan promised. She knew it was important both to accept a friend's gift and to give one in return. Sarah and Joseph lived modern lives, but they were as proud as their ancestors. Megan was deeply touched by the gift. If Juanita had made it for her own wedding, it was almost eighty-five years old and carried some of the family's magic with it.

Joseph opened her car door, and Megan hugged Sarah before she got in. "I'll be back soon."

They waved as she backed into the side yard to turn around and drove down the rutted road that led back to the highway and town.

Chapter Eleven

During his lunch break Reid drove to see Chad. The secretary nodded to him and waved him into Chad's private office.

"Reid! Good to see you. I've been trying to call you. Your secretary said you were out of town but wouldn't tell me where."

"Megan and I spent a week in Florida. You ought to go to Vero Beach, Chad. It's great."

"And take Alice? I doubt I'd enjoy that as much as you quite obviously enjoyed it with Megan. How is she? Want to get together soon?"

"She's wonderful, and we'd like to do that." He sat in a leather chair and slid low on his spine to regard his friend. "There's something I want to tell you."

Chad had been glancing through his appointment calendar looking for an open evening, but the tone of Reid's voice got his full attention. "Oh? What's that?"

"Megan and I are getting married." Reid could no longer pretend to be solemn, and his grin spread from ear to ear. "We told Terry and Jeanette last night."

"Married!" Chad sat back, looking stunned. "How did they take it?"

"You know how kids are," Reid said with a shrug. "They were surprised."

"So am I! I thought you said that you had no intention of remarrying, and neither had Megan. What happened to merely living together?"

"We changed our minds."

"Are you sure about this?"

"We aren't two teenagers planning to elope before our parents catch us. Of course we're sure."

"Since when does maturity mean infallible decision making?"

Reid's smile faded. "You aren't taking this the way I expected. I thought you'd be pleased for us."

"I just hate to see you jump into something so permanent. What's the rush?"

Reid's voice cooled, and his words became clipped. "The rush is that I love her and she loves me, and we're both forty years old. Why the hell should we wait?"

Chad made a calming motion with his hands and came around the desk to sit in the chair next to Reid. "Take it easy. I don't have anything against Megan. The more I hear of her, the more I think she's right for you."

"Then I have your blessing, Father?" Reid asked with a frown. "Damn it, Chad, I wasn't looking for your permission!"

"Why are you yelling at me? All I did was ask if you knew what you were doing. Why are you so defensive?"

"I'm sorry. The truth is that the girls didn't take it well at all. They were as rude as I've ever seen them, in fact.

They're just kids—I know that—but I expected more from them. And from you. Damn it, you're my best friend. Can't you be supportive?''

"Sorry, pal. I guess it's part of being a lawyer. I keep looking for hidden motives and getting suspicious. I like Megan, and I know she's getting a great guy.''

"I wish you'd said that to start with. Pamela went all to pieces over it, just as I knew she would. She threatened to never let me see the girls again.''

"She can't do that. You have legal visitation rights.''

"Legally she can't, but you hear of it happening every day. You know, maybe I'm naive, but I thought when two consenting adults decided to get married, it was a simple thing. I mean, you ask the lady, she accepts, you get married. Right? Wrong. It's not that simple at all.''

"I know. I even used to think that once I grew up I'd make my own decisions, but I have Alice and a senior law partner, and my secretary would just love to do my thinking for me, too.''

Reid gave him a weak grin and sighed. "No matter how difficult all this is, we aren't going to back down. I called the church this morning and arranged to get the chapel the first Saturday in November. Will you be my best man?''

"Do you think I'd stand back and let anyone else be? Of course I'll be your best man.''

"I knew I could count on you. And don't worry about my having rushed into this. Sometimes you just know. There's a feeling deep down in your gut that says, 'Do it, and do it now.' You know? I had that same feeling just before I made the decision to start producing my own line of sporting goods. A decision, I should remind you, that resulted in my netting all this money you're so worried about.''

"Then go with it. I can't argue with success. And, Reid, you are getting a terrific woman."

Reid grinned and nodded. "I know."

Reid had tried to reach Megan all day, and by the time his afternoon meeting was over he was definitely concerned. She wasn't at her house or his apartment, and she had had more than enough time to shop at her usual haunts. As soon as he could, Reid drove to her house, and when she didn't answer the doorbell, he used his key to go in.

Without Megan there, the house seemed quiet and cold. He saw that the thermostat had been turned down to a maintenance level. Megan might do that if she were going out of town. He frowned as he went upstairs. Her bedroom was as empty as the others, and the bed had been neatly made. He was almost glad, for he had begun to have waking nightmares that she might have somehow fallen and hit her head.

Reason took over, and his check of the medicine cabinet in the bathroom showed that her brush and hair dryer were gone. She must have left town, but why? And where?

He sat on the end of the bed and thought. Why would she leave without telling him? Hastily he concluded that she could have one reason: she was getting cold feet about the marriage.

Reid picked up Megan's book of personal phone numbers from beside the bed and began calling each one that seemed likely. However, no one had seen Megan or had any idea where she might have gone. Reid was frustrated and worried but not discouraged. For her to have run away like this, she must be very frightened and confused. He couldn't bear to think she might be alone somewhere, feeling like that.

Deciding she might have left some clue in the small room that she used as an office, Reid poked around in the jumble of papers on her cluttered desk. Three books had been removed from the crowded shelves that lined the room, and he passed over them twice before it occurred to him to read their titles. All three dealt with Indians.

That triggered a memory. Megan had said she wanted to write a book about Indians. When he was upset he always buried himself in work—no doubt she did the same. Perhaps she had gone to interview someone and had had car trouble, or even a wreck. He recalled how remotely located the mountain people were that she had introduced him to, and he groaned. She might freeze out there if she were hurt or stranded! Or maybe she had run into trouble with the people she was interviewing.

He sat down in her desk chair and tried to recall any town or person she might have mentioned. Only one name came to him—Idaho Springs.

Hurrying back down the hall to the bedroom, he dialed information. Using his telephone credit card, he contacted every hotel and motel in town. She was registered at the last one on his list. Reid had the desk clerk ring her room, but no one answered.

He hung up and frowned at the phone. He still didn't know why she was there for certain. She might have gone there to talk to someone, but why wouldn't she simply have used the phone? Maybe she really was running from the idea of marriage. At any rate, it was late, and he doubted there was a surplus of nightlife in Idaho Springs, so why wasn't she in her room? And if nothing was wrong, why hadn't she left a message with Miss Bain at his office?

Reid went back to his car and drove in the direction of Denver and Idaho Springs.

Megan reached the motel later than she had expected, having missed the turn onto the highway in the dark. Knowing the small restaurant at the motel would be closed, she'd stopped at a convenience store and bought cheese, crackers and a bottle of wine.

She was tired by the time she reached her room. She left the sack of food on the Formica table, then showered and put on her robe. With a contented smile, she dried her hair and sat on the bed to call Reid and let him know where she was. There was no answer at his place, so she tried her house. On the fifth ring her answering machine came on, and Megan hung up. She had no desire to talk to her own machine. She wondered where Reid might be, but she wasn't overly concerned. No doubt he had gone grocery shopping or over to Chad's house. She would try him again later.

She sat at the table and propped her bare feet on a second chair as she opened the wine. For a minute she considered turning on the television but decided she was too tired to walk across the room. Perhaps remembering didn't tire Grannie Juanita, but Megan was worn out.

With a paring knife, she sliced a sliver of golden cheese to go with a cracker and slouched low in the chair as she chewed it. She had laid the beaded medallion Grannie Juanita had given her on the table, and as she ate she studied it more closely. Not only did it have great sentimental value, it was of museum quality. She hoped her opal necklace was an equal gift. She was still touched that the old woman had wanted her to have it.

When the banging sounded on her door, Megan jumped and dropped the cracker she was holding. "Who's there?" she demanded as her heart raced.

"Open up, Megan. It's me."

She yanked open the door. "Reid! What's wrong? Why are you here? Has something happened?"

He caught her up in a bear hug and held her tightly against him. "There's no reason to run away, darling. You can talk to me. We'll work it out," he said in a rush.

Pulling back, Megan said, "What? I don't know what you're talking about."

Reid pushed the door shut and looked at the bottle of wine on the table. "Megan, are you all right?"

"Of course I am," she said with a laugh. "Are you?"

"The wine?" he asked almost accusingly.

"I'm eating supper. Want some cheese and crackers? There's another glass in the kitchenette."

For a long minute he stared at her. "You're all right? You aren't running away from me?"

"What? Where did you get an idea like that?"

"Do you mean to tell me that I tore off down here, got two speeding tickets, was worried half out of my mind, and you're all right?" His voice rose until he was almost shouting.

"Good heavens, Reid, do you wish I weren't? Why on earth would you think I had run away?"

"Why didn't you call Miss Bain?"

"Make sense. What does she have to do with this?"

"You should have left a message. For God's sake, Megan, I didn't know what had happened to you!"

"I'm sorry. I tried to call, but you didn't answer. I tried again just a few minutes ago. It never occurred to me that you might worry."

"Not worry? Of course I was worried!"

She put her arms around him and stood on tiptoe to kiss his chin. "I'm sorry. I guess I'm so accustomed to being alone that I didn't think things through. I won't do it again."

"If you're not running away from me, why are you here?" He gestured at the motel room as if it were the end of the earth.

"I came down to interview the Antelopes. Don't look at me like that. I mean Sarah and Joseph Antelope and his grandmother, Juanita. For my book. Remember?"

Reid pulled her close and held her for a long time without speaking. "Honey, don't ever scare me like this again."

"Why would you ever think I might be running away from you? I love you."

"I know you're worried about getting married again. I thought..."

"If I were having cold feet, I'd talk to you, not leave town. For goodness' sake, Reid. Give me credit for having some sense."

"Then you're not backing out and getting ready to ditch me?"

She laughed. "Maybe you should be the writer. You have the imagination for it. Reid, listen to me, and pay attention. I don't have any intention of leaving you or of calling off the wedding. Look. We even got a wedding gift." She reached for the necklace and held it up for his view. "Isn't it beautiful? I'm going to wear it on our wedding day."

Reid admired the necklace, but he was still too concerned about Megan to give it his full attention. "You aren't going to do this regularly, are you? Just take off, I mean? If I had known where you were, I wouldn't have been worried. Well, at least not as much. Maybe I could come with you when you're going up into the mountains."

"Would you like to? That would be wonderful." She beamed at him as she got a glass and poured him some wine. "I'd love to have you along. Since you're here, there are some people I want you to meet—the family I visited today. Especially the grandmother. She's very old—she doesn't even know her exact age. I was afraid you wouldn't get to meet her. Winters are hard in the mountains. Let me tell you about this necklace." She sat cross-legged in the chair as she started telling him about her day.

Reid only half listened. He was almost overwhelmed with relief to find her safe and happy. He decided that life with Megan might be a lot of things, but it would never be dull.

Chapter Twelve

"Reid, what are we ever going to do with all this stuff?"
Megan held up their two blenders and waved them at him
before putting them on the table with the two toasters,
two bean pots and two waffle irons. "You don't happen
to have a set of mixing bowls in these boxes, do you?"

"No, I don't cook that much."

"Darn. I could have used those." Megan waded
through the sea of crumpled newspaper and perched on
the countertop to rest. "How long have we been doing
this? Days?"

Reid consulted his watch. "About four hours."

"Seems longer. Why did I ever think all our things
would fit in my house?"

"Be glad we aren't trying to cram it all into my apartment. We'll get the important things in, keep the better
of our duplicates and get rid of the rest."

"Can you reach the refrigerator? I'd give anything for a soda right now."

"Anything?" Reid said with a melodramatic leer. "One soda coming right up." He maneuvered through the boxes to the refrigerator and then over to sit beside her on the counter. "This really is a mess, isn't it?"

"As long as no one rings the front doorbell, we're all right. Your couch is blocking the entry."

"How are things coming along upstairs?"

"Don't ask. That's why I came down to unpack in the kitchen."

"I told you not to redo the wallpaper until we got settled in."

"I wanted everything to look right, and I just couldn't see you dressing every morning amid lilacs and rosebuds. The blue and camel stripes look much better with your bedspread. Do you think Jeanette and Terry will like their rooms?" A note of worry crept into her voice.

"They'd better, or I'll wring their necks," he said cheerfully. "You've worked your rear end off up there."

"You know, I like you. I love you, too, but I really like you as well."

"Thanks, buddy."

Megan laughed. "Back to work. At this rate we won't be finished by the time of the wedding, and our friends will have to sit on boxes." She slid off the counter and kicked aside paper to make room to bring in another box. "Honey, it wasn't necessary to wrap all the canned goods in newspaper."

"I was on a roll."

She tried to lift a deceptively small box but couldn't budge it. "What on earth do you have in here?"

"My weights! I've been looking everywhere for them."
He picked up the box as easily as if it contained cotton
balls and carried it toward the stairs.

Megan watched him with a fond smile. The wedding
was only a week away, and they had decided that he
should move in now rather than pay another month's
rent on his apartment for only a few days' use. She
wished she had agreed to live with him weeks earlier.
They had been together every night anyway, and by now
they would have been finished with the moving.

"I never knew a bachelor could accumulate so much
stuff!" she called to him. "I thought you all lived
threadbare existences."

"I've been collecting junk so you'd have lots to do,"
he yelled back. "If you're busy, you won't have time to
consider backing out."

"At this rate, I'll be lucky if I'm finished before we're
grandparents." She stacked his canned goods with her
own in the pantry and wondered what on earth Reid liked
to eat that involved so many tins of pitted olives. Some
of the bottled sauces were a mystery to her as well. She
held up one as Reid came back to the kitchen. "What's
this?"

"Pepper sauce. Don't you like spicy food?"

"Sure, but this looks lethal." She bent to put the bottle on a lower shelf.

Reid smiled at the sight of her rounded posterior. "You
look better in tight jeans than anyone I ever saw. In fact,
you look better out of them, as well."

She swiveled to give him a mock threatening look. "I
see that gleam in your eye, and you can forget it. We'll
never get you moved in at this rate."

He made a show of striding toward her through the wads of newspaper as if they were drifts of heavy snow, his fingers curled as if he meant to pounce on her.

"Now, Reid." Megan laughed as she sidestepped him. "I haven't got time to fool with you."

He gave a villainous laugh and pretended to twirl the end of an imaginary moustache. "Come to me, my little litchi nut, and I'll make your day."

"You made my day this morning." She laughed as she dodged him again. Turning, she ran toward the living room, skirting endless boxes.

Reid jumped the boxes and caught up with her at the couch. He tumbled her onto the cushions and buried his chin into the ticklish part of her neck as he deftly unbuttoned her blouse. Megan shrieked and swatted at him. Reid pulled open her blouse and nuzzled the valley between her breasts.

The sound of the doorbell made them both jerk their heads around to stare toward the entry. "Who could that be?" she asked.

"I don't know. It's your house."

She scrambled out from under him and hurriedly rebuttoned her blouse, then tried to smooth her tumbled hair as she climbed over the couch. When she opened the door and found Pamela on the porch, her smile died. As usual Pamela looked as if a couturier had just finished with her. Megan pulled her loose shirttail straight. "Hello, Pamela. What brings you here?"

"I must talk to you. It's about Reid. Before you marry him, I think you should know what sort of man he is."

"I already do."

"Not as well as I do. After all, I lived with him for eighteen years. And it wasn't easy. He's cold and selfish and will pay more attention to that job of his than he will to you."

Megan tried to keep a straight face and hoped all her buttons were fastened and her cheeks not too flushed. "Thank you for telling me. Was there anything else?"

"If I could just come in for a few minutes..."

"Well, as you can see, the place is quite a mess right now. Perhaps some other time."

"Hello, Pamela," Reid said as he shoved the couch back out of the way. "What else did you want to say about me?"

Pamela gave Megan an accusing glare. "You didn't tell me he was here. And why are you moving now? The girls said you aren't getting married for another week."

"You can figure that out," he said brusquely.

"Yes. I suppose I can." Fat tears welled up in Pamela's eyes, and she looked totally vulnerable.

Reid frowned. How had he ever been foolish enough to be taken in by this show of helplessness? He knew Pamela to be as tough as a marine when she was after something she wanted. "That won't work anymore," he said wearily.

"What, Reid?" she asked in a wispy, feminine voice.

Megan looked at her in confusion. She cried with such difficulty herself that she was concerned that Pamela might be truly heartbroken. "Do you want a glass of water or something? I don't know where the coffeepot is right now."

"If I could just sit down for a bit and talk to you," Pamela said wistfully. "I won't take much of your time. After all, if you're going to marry Reid, I think we ought to get to know each other."

"I don't see why—"

"Now, Reid, a few minutes won't hurt," Megan said as she stepped back from the door. "Come in, Pamela."

Pamela walked daintily into the jumbled living room and sat uneasily on the edge of the couch. She didn't comment, but her disgusted expression was eloquent.

Megan sat in a chair, and Reid perched on the arm next to her, unconsciously making himself and Megan a unit against Pamela, the outsider. "Why do you need to talk to us?"

"If the girls are going to be coming here—and my lawyer says I must give you visitation rights—I want to know what sort of a place it is. Will they have a bedroom to sleep in?"

"Of course," Megan said, "Each of the girls will have a room of her own."

"Upstairs, I suppose? Where is . . . your room?"

"Across the hall."

Pamela wiped at a new batch of tears and tried to look brave. Reid clenched his jaw in an effort to remain civil.

"Is there a yard?"

"Yes."

"The girls are a little old to need a yard to play in, Pamela," he pointed out dryly.

"They mentioned something about a pool?"

"We talked to them about putting one in," Megan said. "So far it's just an idea."

"It must be nice," Pamela said with a resigned sigh. "I wouldn't know, myself."

"Cut out the poor-me act," Reid broke in abruptly. "You aren't hard up for money."

"Reid, how could you possibly know about my finances?" she chided gently. "Megan, you understand, of course, that I can't allow the girls to come over until their rooms are ready? All this is so difficult for them as it is.

Naturally it's out of the question until after the wedding. I must shield them as well as I can."

"We would hardly be doing anything objectionable around them," Megan answered with diminishing patience. "We don't have anything decadent planned. No orgies or anything."

Pamela merely gave her a doubtful look.

Reid stood and said, "You're being insulting, Pamela. I think it's time you left."

"I suppose. Before I bring the the girls over, I'll check back with you to see that everything is in order."

"That's not necessary. I'll pick them up in time for us all to go to the church."

"No, no. I'll bring them."

"You're coming to the wedding?" Megan exclaimed. "I mean, that seems a bit irregular."

"Why shouldn't I? My daughters are going to be in it. I had no choice in that, but I do have the right to see them there and home safely. After all," she added to Reid, "you were glad to see me at your other wedding."

Megan swallowed nervously. This was getting out of hand. "There *is* a difference."

"Is there, Reid? How do you feel? Would you bar me from a wedding our daughters are in? If you're really getting married, why shouldn't I be allowed to witness it?"

"Why would you want to?" Megan asked.

"No. That's final." Reid took Pamela's arm and steered her efficiently toward the door. "I'm going to pick up the girls at seven o'clock. You aren't coming to the church."

"We'll see about that, Reid!" Pamela snapped as she jerked her arm away and dropped her act of helpless femininity. "We'll just see about that!"

Megan jumped as the door slammed behind the woman, and she stared wide-eyed at Reid. "What did she mean by that? Does that mean she'll be there or that the girls won't be?"

"It will work out just fine," Reid growled protectively. "I'll see to that."

Megan gladly went into the security of his embrace, but she wasn't at all convinced.

Chapter Thirteen

It's still raining," Reid said as he paced nervously to the window.

"In some cultures it's considered lucky to have rain on a wedding day. It's supposed to be a symbol of fertility and abundance and that sort of thing."

"Here it's a sign of slick streets and possibly sleet by morning."

"Everything will be fine. The wedding will be over long before the streets ice up." Megan put the last pin in her hair and picked up her hand mirror so she could see to put the spray of baby's breath in her hair. "I thought the bride was the one who was supposed to be nervous."

"Maybe I should call the girls to be certain they're going to be ready."

Megan took her dress out of the closet and stepped into it. "Will you zip me up?" she asked as she pulled the soft-pink wool sleeves over her arms.

Reid raised the zipper and fastened the hidden hook at the top. "I still can't believe the church secretary booked two weddings for the same night."

"We only wanted the chapel anyway. What difference does it make?"

"And it's raining. You'll get wet."

"I have a raincoat and an umbrella."

"I'd better call the girls. With the preacher going straight to the other wedding, we can't afford to be late."

With an indulgent smile, Megan nodded. "Tell them we'll be there in fifteen minutes."

For the hundredth time Reid glanced at his watch, looked at the damp windowpanes and groaned. He sat on the bed to dial Pamela's number.

Megan studied her reflection in the cheval mirror. Her dress was elegantly simple, with a collar that hugged her neck, long sleeves that tapered to her arms and wrists, and a softly swirling gored skirt that barely skimmed the floor. The pink wool was as soft as cotton candy and looked almost as delicate. She fastened small silver earrings in her ears and ceremoniously took out the intricate beaded necklace and looped it over her head. The effect was both unique and stunning.

As Reid hung up the phone, Megan stepped into her heels and took his suit coat off the hanger to hold it for him. He shrugged into it and stepped back to say, "How do I look?"

"Like a man on his way to a hanging. Will you calm down?" She laughed as she smoothed her hand over his coat and straightened his tie. "For someone who's been so worried about my backing out, you're certainly nervous about this."

"You aren't going to change your mind at the last minute, are you? This is a big step, you know."

"Yes, darling, I know. I'm not going to change my mind. Are you?"

"No way." He grinned and tried hard to look more relaxed. "Turn around and let me look at you. God, Megan, you're beautiful. I even like the necklace, though I have to admit that I had my doubts about it until now."

He took their raincoats from the closet and helped Megan into hers. "I had hoped for a perfect night."

"Quit worrying. It is a perfect night. It's just raining, that's all."

"Why are you so calm all of a sudden? All week you've been as nervous as a thief."

"We can't both have nervous breakdowns at once," she teased. "Do you have my ring?"

Reid fished in his suit pocket and produced a red-velvet box. Opening it, he showed her the band glistening with diamonds, then put it back into his pocket.

"And the marriage license?"

He patted his inside pocket. "I have it."

"I have your ring. I guess we'd better go."

Reid drove the car close to the kitchen door, and Megan dashed out under cover of the umbrella as he leaned across to open her door. She watched him with amusement as he drove toward Pamela's house. "It's a good thing you don't get married often. I don't think you could stand it."

"You're right. This is it! We'd better make a go of it, because I can't stand the strain." He glanced at her and winked as his teeth flashed in a smile.

Pamela's house was large and sat among others of an equally impressive size. Megan peered through the night to see the carefully landscaped lawn and the formal lines of the house. "Nice," she commented as Reid drove up the broad drive.

"I never cared for it. The design is too stylish for comfort."

She had almost forgotten that he had once lived here. The house's beauty paled as she pictured him here with Pamela. Perhaps, she thought, the jealousy wasn't as dead as she had hoped. Megan felt rather odd sitting in Pamela's drive with Reid. Again she reflected on the complexities involved in a second marriage.

Reid sounded the horn, and the side door opened. Pamela stood there for a minute as if she were barring the door with her body. Megan felt cold all over. Pamela wasn't dressed like a woman who planned to spend the evening alone at home. Nervousness spread through her as she waited to see what Pamela would do. Then Pamela stepped aside, and Terry and Jeanette came through the covered walk and got into the back seat of the car.

Vastly relieved, Megan turned in the seat to look at them. "You both look so pretty. That's a new hairstyle, isn't it, Terry?"

Terry nodded sullenly. Jeanette stared through the side window.

"Did your dresses fit okay?" Megan asked in an effort to induce conversation.

"I guess," Jeanette said in a bored voice. "Rose isn't exactly my favorite color."

"It was last week," Reid said, glancing at his younger daughter in the rearview mirror.

"I changed my mind."

"I never intend to wear rose again," Terry stated in a voice that dripped with self-pity. "Never as long as I live."

As Reid backed into the street, Megan again saw Pamela silhouetted in the bright doorway, her stance one of a woman watching a personal disaster being enacted before her eyes. Terry had evidently learned her melodramatics by observing her mother.

They reached the church without incident, though a few minutes later than intended, and Reid parked in the covered drive. The parking lot was full.

The chapel was in a quiet part of the building behind the main sanctuary. As they made their way through the crowd of people waiting for the second wedding, they were met with several obvious frowns from those who thought this inconvenience was either her fault or Reid's. Megan simply ignored them. Nothing was going to spoil this day for her.

When they arrived at the chapel, their friends were already seated, whispering quietly among themselves. Reid took their coats into the small vestibule while Megan helped the girls straighten their dresses. She smiled warmly at them as she whispered encouragingly, "You both look beautiful. Do you remember what to do? Just walk down the aisle one at a time and stand on the left. After we're finished, you walk up the aisle with Chad."

"We aren't dummies," Terry snapped. "Of course we know what to do."

Megan gave Terry a level look and wondered if she would ever feel a closeness with her. Since they had announced their wedding plans, Jeanette had been as difficult as Terry. Megan took her borrowed prayer book and arranged the thick blue ribbon in the pages. For something new she had her dress, and the something old was, of course, Juanita's necklace.

Reid returned, smiling his approval at the sight of the three people he loved more dearly than anything in the world. Megan was a picture of loveliness, and his daughters looked so grown up. He reassuringly squeezed Megan's hand, then signaled the organist that they were

ready. As soon as the music began, the murmurs died
down, and Reid joined Chad, who was his best man, at
the altar rail.

"That Indian thing looks really weird," Jeanette hissed
as the music changed to the processional march. Before
Megan could reply, Jeanette started down the aisle.

Terry smiled faintly and followed her sister. By the time
she was in view of the congregation, however, her smile
had disappeared, and she looked the part of the vestal
virgin on her way to the sacrifice. Wishing she could swat
them both, Megan lifted her chin and began the short
walk to Reid's side.

As she moved slowly toward the altar, Megan saw the
preacher shifting his weight from one foot to the other,
obviously anxious to finish this ceremony so he could get
on to the next wedding. But she would not be hurried.
Reid's eyes met hers with an outpouring of the love he
felt for her, and she was doubly reassured that this was
the right thing to do. In a few short minutes her life would
be joined with his, and she knew it would be forever. His
ring was warm in the palm of her hand beneath the prayer
book. Soon she would be placing it on his finger as a vis-
ible sign of their love. Reid reached out and took her
hand as she moved to his side. She was ready to put Megan Wayne aside and become Megan Spencer.

Terry and Jeanette took their places beside Megan,
Jeanette looking thoroughly bored and Terry like a lamb
ready for the ax. Megan was greatly relieved that Pamela hadn't come after all. Up until this point she had
been afraid the woman would show up and cause a painful scene. But the doors of the chapel had been shut by
the ushers after Megan's entrance, and Pamela was not
to be seen.

"Dearly beloved," the preacher began. The familiar words seemed fresh and new to Megan as she heard them applied to Reid and herself. Yes, she would honor and cherish him, stand by him in sickness and in health.

The preacher asked if anyone had cause to object to their marriage, and Megan smiled up at Reid in the brief silence. Then the preacher began the final vows.

Suddenly Terry screamed and bent double, clutching her middle. Megan jumped and stared at the girl. Terry's eyes were clenched shut, and her face was contorted as horrible moans, signaling excruciating pain, came from her open mouth. Jeanette screamed and pressed both her hands to her face in horror.

Reid brushed past Megan to embrace Terry. "Terry? Honey, what's wrong?"

"I'm sorry, Dad. Ooh, the pain!"

Megan knelt before the girl and said, "What pain? Where does it hurt?"

"All over!" Terry pressed her face against Reid's suit coat as the murmurs of the congregation rose.

"Is she all right?" the preacher asked anxiously.

"She's dying!" Jeanette wailed. "Terry's dying!"

Reid tried to disengage Terry's tightly clasped arms from around her middle. "Does it hurt here? How about here?" He gently tried to probe the area above her appendix.

Terry shrieked and bent lower.

"Is it her appendix?" Megan asked. "How could it get this bad so quickly? She was perfectly fine a minute ago."

"I haven't felt well all day," Terry groaned. "I didn't tell you because I didn't want you to worry, Dad." With a loud moan, she added, "Go on with the wedding. Don't mind me."

Shock poured through Megan. Terry was acting! She wasn't in pain at all! "Reid, I think—"

"We have to get her to the hospital," he interrupted.

"The hospital!" Jeanette shrieked. "I knew she was dying!"

"Jeanette, hush!" Megan put her hand on Reid's. "Let me see." Megan reached over and lightly touched Terry's abdomen. "If it's her appendix, her stomach will feel tight, and it doesn't seem to be—"

"Don't poke so hard!" Terry cried out. "Dad, don't let her hurt me!"

By now the whole congregation was crowding around the altar in alarm. Megan snapped her mouth shut to hold back the words she was so close to saying. She had caught Terry's eyes for a moment and knew the girl was faking. To say so, however, was out of the question. To even suggest she might be exaggerating would seal her fate with Reid's friends and maybe even create a permanent rift between herself and Reid. With difficulty Megan stood and said coolly, "Yes, Reid. Perhaps we should take her to the hospital."

Chad eased over close to Reid and asked in the reverential tone one usually reserved for funerals, "Should I call Pamela?"

"Mom! I want my mother," Terry sobbed. "Please, Dad, can I see my mother?"

"Call her and tell her to meet us in the emergency room," Reid told Chad. "Since she has legal custody, she'll have to be there to sign the papers."

"I can't walk," Terry wailed as she saw Reid exchange an apologetic look with Megan.

"She looks awful," Jeanette sobbed, her always available tears flowing in profusion.

Megan looked from one girl to the other, then back at Reid. Why couldn't he see this was all a pretense? "Reid, I don't think . . ."

"You're right," he said, misinterpreting her meaning. "She can't walk." He scooped Terry up in his arms and carried her purposefully through the crowd. Jeanette clung to his arm, and Megan had to hurry to keep up with them. As the crowd parted to let them pass, Megan heard speculations and commiseration for Terry on every side.

When they were in the car and Reid was running around to get in behind the wheel, Megan looked over her shoulder, her eyes meeting Terry's. For a brief instant the girl's expression was one of triumph, her face free from contortions and her eyes almost laughing. But when Reid got into the car, her grimacing and moaning resumed.

Reid's strong face was pale with worry, and he drove to the hospital as fast as possible, speeding down the dark, rain-washed streets and taking corners in a squeal of tires. At the hospital emergency entrance, he skidded the car to a stop and ran around to carry Terry in. Jeanette got out, too, and while they rushed inside, Megan parked the car. As she headed toward the building, pulling her coat tightly around her against the cold wind, the drizzle suddenly became a downpour, drenching her from head to toe.

Inside, the brightly lit hospital smelled of antiseptic and medicine. The nurse at the desk eyed Megan's appearance disapprovingly, then indicated the direction in which Reid had taken the girls. As Megan hurried after them, she heard the nurse barking instructions to an orderly to mop up the hall before someone slipped and got hurt.

Terry lay curled on a narrow bed, with Jeanette and Reid trying to soothe her. When Megan came in, he cast a worried look in her direction, then went back to comforting his daughter. Megan surveyed the scene in silence. She didn't trust herself to say a word. With a towel from a nearby table, Megan dried her hair and face and the hem of her wedding dress. Most of her makeup came off on the towel, but she could do nothing about that now.

A moment later, Pamela raced into the room, casting a brief glance at Megan, then threw herself across Terry. "My baby," she sobbed. "What's happened? What's the matter with her?"

"She's dying!" Jeanette hiccupped. By now her tears had evolved into subdued sobs.

"It may be her appendix," Reid said as he stroked Terry's dark hair.

Pamela put her hand on Reid's arm as if she needed his strength. "My baby! My poor baby!"

Megan's head tilted to one side as she tried to determine whether Pamela was part of the charade or if this entire production was the girls' idea. The concern on her face looked real, but Megan wasn't sure. Reid was ignoring Pamela and didn't seem to notice that she still had her hand on his arm. Again Megan wondered about the way Pamela was dressed. She must have been anticipating leaving the house. Otherwise she wouldn't have been so elegantly attired.

Feeling completely helpless and totally out of place, Megan turned and went to the small waiting room opposite the nurses' station. The nurse she had encountered earlier looked up from her paperwork and gave Megan an appraising stare, as if she wondered what Megan's part was in all this and why she showed no signs of worry or hysteria. Megan couldn't have explained if she had wanted to.

Megan sat on one of the uncomfortable vinyl chairs and pushed away an ashtray that reeked of old cigarettes. She had rarely been this angry, and she was surprised that she was containing her feelings so well. Realizing she still clutched Reid's wedding band, Megan methodically removed the velvet ring box from her purse, placed the ring inside, put the box back in the purse, then with a snap closed her purse and folded her arms over it, pulling it tightly against her. Crossing her legs, Megan studied her dress and heels. They were probably ruined, she reflected. Just like the wedding. She had the curious sensation of being outside herself, an observer.

Leaning forward, Megan peered down the hall. A man who must be the doctor was entering the emergency room. In a few minutes Jeanette came out and joined Megan in the waiting room. Megan made no comment as the girl dropped into a chair opposite her. She knew the girl was glaring at her, but she remained cool and aloof.

"I'm surprised you're still here," Jeanette said, breaking the long silence. "You ought to take Dad's car and leave."

Megan didn't answer.

"Mom will take him home."

The nurse looked up sharply and stared again at Megan. Megan ignored her.

"We don't need you here," Jeanette tried again.

"Why are you doing this?" Megan said at last.

"Doing what? I'm not doing anything." Jeanette slumped sullenly into the chair, looking away from Megan.

Megan continued to stare at Jeanette until the girl began to squirm and at last met Megan's eyes. "You two have managed to ruin what was to have been the happiest event of our lives. Doesn't it bother you that your dad will be hurt by this?''

"I don't know what you're talking about. Terry can't help it if she got sick. You wouldn't care if she died!"

"There's nothing wrong with Terry, and you know it as well as I do." Megan continued to speak calmly, but there was a razor-sharp edge to her voice.

"My mom was right! You don't care anything about us! You hate us!"

"No, I don't hate you. I don't love you, either, though I had hoped to someday. In order to be loved, you have to be lovable."

Jeanette's chin trembled, and tears filled her eyes again.

"Are those real? It's hard to tell."

"You're heartless and cruel!"

"And what about yourself?" Megan shook her head slowly. "I hope someday you learn to think for yourself. Terry probably had this idea, and as usual you followed wherever she led. This time you've gone too far. I hope for your sake as well as for your father's that he never finds out the truth about what happened tonight. No, I'm not going to tell him. If he believes this farce and I say Terry is faking, it might come between us. And, Jeanette, nobody is going to do that." Megan hadn't raised her voice or spoken in anything but the calmest tone, but Jeanette seemed to shrivel beneath her stare.

In Terry's room, Reid anxiously watched the doctor press Terry's lower abdomen while Pamela cried quietly and looked more miserable than her daughter.

"Does this hurt?" the doctor asked.

"No, sir," Terry said meekly. "I guess whatever was wrong has stopped."

"Do appendixes do that?" Pamela asked pitifully.

"Not as a rule."

Reid looked more closely at Terry. She was pale, but she was no longer screaming at the slightest touch. She was even able to straighten out and lie flat on her back.

The doctor stopped poking at her and perused her as if he wasn't quite sure what to make of her. Silently he put his stethoscope to her chest and listened to her heartbeat.

"Is she all right?" Reid asked.

"She seems fine. I don't see any sign of appendicitis or anything else that might be wrong."

"Thank God!" Pamela exclaimed as if her child had been reprieved from certain death.

"Then I'll be okay?" Terry asked in a weak voice.

"Unless it flares up again in the next few minutes, I see no reason to keep you here."

Reid noticed Terry was pointedly avoiding his eyes, and the first real suspicion entered his mind. "What exactly happened at the church, Terry?"

"Why, you saw it, Dad. I nearly passed out with pain. I've never felt anything like it!"

Reid made no comment, but his eyes narrowed.

Pamela raised her head, her eyes wide and filled with dread. "Are you... That is, did the wedding take place?"

"No, Mom. All this happened right after the preacher asked if anyone objected."

Even as realization gradually stole over Reid, he fought it. "You remember exactly what was happening just before you had this attack? Then it certainly must have come on fast."

"Yes, Dad. It did."

"Almost as fast as it went away." His eyes met the doctor's, and Reid saw veiled amusement there.

"I've never seen anything like it," Terry said.

"Yes. You said that already." To the doctor, Reid said, "You don't find anything wrong at all?"

"Not a thing. If I were you, I'd take her home and put her to bed for the rest of the evening, but if she feels fine tomorrow, I'd say there's nothing wrong with her." To Terry he said, "You won't miss any school, I'm afraid."

"I'm glad," she said meekly. "I love school."

Pamela beamed at her through her tears and murmured something about her being such a good girl.

Reid's mouth tightened, and a muscle in his jaw clenched. "I'll call you tomorrow, Terry. We have a lot to talk about."

"Yes, Dad."

Turning on his heel, Reid strode from the room. When he reached the waiting area, he stared at Jeanette, who was already looking thoroughly miserable.

"How is Terry?" Megan asked.

"She's fine." He continued to frown at his younger daughter. "Well, Jeanette?"

"I'm glad Terry is going to live."

He bit back his anger at her much-too-innocent voice. Taking a deep breath, he steadied himself. Megan must never know that his daughters might have deliberately sabotaged their wedding. "Your mother and Terry will be out soon to take you home."

Megan stood up, put her rain-soaked coat back on and slipped her purse beneath her coat to keep it dry. Without a word between them, she went with Reid into the night.

Time seemed to have stopped for Megan as they drove silently through the streets. All this had an air of surrealism, as though it had been a bad dream. Megan tried to determine Reid's thoughts from his expression as she stole a glance or two, but she could not read him. He seemed very far away. Before she could stop herself, she asked, "What was the doctor's diagnosis?"

"He said he wasn't sure but that she seemed to have recovered from whatever it might have been."

"Maybe it was just nerves."

Reid looked over at her in the dark. Was Megan sincere, or did she know the truth? "I'm sorry about tonight, darling. I can't tell you how very sorry I am."

"So am I."

"Is there anything we can do to salvage this night?" he asked.

"We could go home and reassure each other."

"I'll call the preacher tomorrow and set another date."

"Not yet." She still felt curiously detached, as if all this were happening to someone else. "After what happened tonight, I'm not sure we should do this again...so quickly."

"Does that mean you won't marry me?"

"No. I'm not sure what it means. I just need time."

"What exactly does that mean? Do you want me to move back to my apartment?"

"No, I love you. There's no reason we shouldn't live together."

"Pamela said Terry and Jeanette can't come over until we're married," he reminded her. "I don't know if we can see them if we're only living together."

"They we'll see them somewhere else. There are ways to get around that."

Reid frowned. "I love you, Megan. We got off to a false start, but we'll get past this."

She leaned over to kiss his cheek as the first pellets of sleet hissed against the window.

Chapter Fourteen

"Come back to bed, Megan."

She shook her head and touched her forehead to the cool glass. In the thin light of dawn she could see that the first snow of the year had blanketed the yard. Megan curled up on the window seat and pulled the comforter more snugly around her.

Reid got out of bed and went sleepily to the window as he wrapped a quilt around his naked body. "Why not?"

"I don't know. I was thinking."

He sat beside her and ran his fingers through his rumpled hair. "About last night, I suppose. As you said, it must have been nerves." Feeling a great deal of exasperation, Reid breathed a long sigh, then blurted out, "You don't think there was anything wrong with Terry, do you."

"Do you?" Megan said too quickly, then turned to see Reid's beleaguered expression. "I didn't mean that the way it sounded. I'm just feeling hurt that they dislike me so much.''

"They don't know you well enough to decide whether they like you or not.''

Megan didn't respond. At one moment she wished Reid could see his daughters objectively, as she did. The next, she hoped Reid would never know how selfish and cruel they had been. Maybe Pamela had put them up to it. Megan doubted she would ever know for sure. Nevertheless, the girls did spoil the ceremony and were very effectively coming between them. Reid loved them too dearly to see their faults. Megan could only hope that he loved her that much. Pensively she drew a circle in the frost on the windowpane.

"When I was a girl I used to love snow. We had snow in Charlotte but not like we have here. The first year here I was afraid to drive in it."

"Why are you talking about snow?''

"It seems to be a safer subject than your daughters."

"Maybe it was a combination of nerves and Pamela's influence." Reid tried to look hopeful. It was hard for him to accept that the girls were solely responsible. They were his daughters, and he felt very protective of them.

Megan raised her eyebrows before looking back at the snow. "This was to have been our first day as husband and wife." She held out her bare left hand. "Isn't it strange? For so long I put off agreeing to marry you, and right up to yesterday I was as nervous as I could be. Now I feel bereaved because it didn't happen."

"Darling, I feel as married to you as I possibly could."

"Somehow it's not exactly the same thing."

"As soon as the church office opens I'll call the preacher and get a new date set."

"No."

"Megan, that doesn't make any sense. You say you're unhappy because we didn't get married, yet you don't want me to reschedule the ceremony. Will you be reasonable?"

"It won't work, Reid!"

"What do you mean, it won't work? You love me, and I love you. What's not going to work?"

"Don't you see, Reid? It's not just us. We have to consider Jeanette and Terry, too."

"Wait a minute. What do they have to do with our love? What are you saying?" Reid's tone was defensive.

"They ruined our wedding, didn't they?"

"It wasn't Terry's fault. She was just nervous."

"Terry hates me. They both hate me, and you can't see it because you love them too much."

"Love them too much? Are you jealous of my love for my daughters?"

"Don't be ridiculous, Reid! They hate me, you can't see that, and they *are* coming between us! See? They even have us shouting at each other."

For a moment Reid was speechless; then in a gentle voice he said, "Megan. Dear Megan. I love you."

"And I love you, too, Reid. But—"

Reid interrupted her by placing a finger on her lips. "Please don't say any more until I finish." When Megan did as he asked, Reid cleared his throat and continued. "I know all this has been a terrible strain on you. It has been on me, too. Terry and Jeanette really are good kids, and I have a hard time believing that they're intentionally trying to keep us apart."

Megan wanted to tell him how wrong he was and try to get him to see the truth, but she had agreed to let him finish, so she kept her mouth shut.

"You see, Terry and Jeanette have never had to vie for my attention. Even when Pamela and I were married, it was the girls who got my time, not Pamela. My guess is they see you as a threat. If I'm with you, I won't be with them. That's pretty selfish, but they're just kids. And you know what? I'm awfully fond of their attention, too."

Every time Reid spoke of his daughters, Megan could see the undeniable love he felt for them. They had been a very important part of his life for many years, and he had only known her a short time. How could she presume to come between them? She fought back the tears that threatened to form in her eyes.

Reid noticed her pain. "Megan, I know we can work all this out if we just keep our heads. You say you don't want to set a new date for the wedding right now. I understand. Until you feel comfortable with all this, we won't discuss it again. If you want me to move back into my apartment, all you have to do is say the word."

"That's not the problem, Reid. It's not us—it's the girls."

"Yeah, I know. We all need to start over. I've thought of that. We should get away from here for a weekend— onto neutral turf, so to speak—maybe up in the mountains. This is important. We have to pull together."

Megan sighed and nodded her agreement, though she felt that such a weekend would only prolong the agony of their ultimate separation because of his daughters.

Reid reached out to touch the cool skin of her cheek. "Come back to bed, honey. You're getting cold."

Obediently Megan followed him back to the wide bed and let him unwrap her from the comforter. Like Reid, she preferred sleeping in the nude, and as her bare skin met the chill in the air, she hurried to get beneath the covers. She snuggled beside him, and he drew her head onto his shoulder. In the strength of Reid's embrace, Megan felt very secure yet oddly vulnerable.

She put her arm across his broad chest and looked up at him. "Reid. Make love with me."

Without hesitation, Reid gently kissed her, then pulled back to smile at her dewy lips. "You kiss better than anyone else in the world."

"How do you know?" she said with a wan smile. "Have you tried them all?"

"I know by instinct."

She kissed the warm curve of his jaw. "You taste good."

"Keep that up, and it will get you into trouble."

"I like your brand of trouble."

Reid rolled to pin her under him and smiled down at her. "You're even beautiful in the morning."

"Now I know you're in love," she said with a genuine laugh, her worries set aside for the moment.

Encouraged that he had lifted her spirits, Reid said, "You really are. No pillow creases, no blotchy skin. I should keep you in bed all the time."

"That's not a bad idea. Or at least all weekend."

"With brief forays out to build a snowman."

"And make snow ice cream."

He grimaced. "Do you really like snow ice cream?"

"It's a tradition. Every snowfall my mother made some for me. Her mother made it for her, and so on. After a few years it doesn't taste so bad."

"This tastes much better." He ran the tip of his tongue over the mound of her breasts. "And this." Gently he pulled her nipple into his mouth and drew on it sensuously.

Megan murmured and moved beneath him as she arched her body to offer herself to him. Reid complied and loved first one breast, then the other, until both nipples were moist and pouting for his attention. Brushing his palm over the rosy buds, he said, "I love the way you respond to me. You're always as eager as I am."

"I love you. I want you." Megan's full attention was focused on Reid as she let her hands glide down his muscled back to cup his firm buttocks. "You feel so good against me." Moving her hips seductively, she gave him an inviting smile.

Reid shifted so that he knelt between her thighs, but rather than entering her right away, his hand sought out the moist curls there. Megan opened herself to him and relished the exquisite sensation of his knowing fingers upon her and of the heady realization that he was watching her enjoy him.

When she could wait no longer, she urged him into her, and the fullness of his manhood made her cry out as her pleasure peaked and exploded. Reid held her close, murmuring words of love in her ear as waves of physical and emotional bliss swept through her.

When he felt her begin to relax, he started to move within her, slowly at first, then more rapidly. Megan's pulse leaped and seemed to center deep in her loins. She matched his pace, and their mutual desire built toward a roaring crescendo. A guttural moan from deep within Reid signaled that he could no longer contain himself, and that knowledge triggered Megan's release. Their souls merged as the rapture of their union carried them on the crest of its wave.

Later as Megan lay peacefully in his arms, absently stroking his firm torso, unbidden thoughts of their earlier discussion came rushing back to her. She tried to block them, to think of something pleasant, but even her attempts to concentrate on the ecstasy of their lovemaking was to no avail. She had never loved anyone more than Reid Spencer, not even Hugh, and now she was losing Reid as surely as disease had taken Hugh away from her. Did Reid love his daughters more than he loved her? she wondered, then chastised herself for wondering.

Megan looked over at Reid as he slept beside her, his distinguished silvery hair tousled across his forehead. His lips were slightly upturned at the corners as though he might be having a pleasant dream. She couldn't help envying his apparent peacefulness.

She loved Reid, but would she be able to let him go if it came to that? She wasn't sure. But she was certain about one thing. She didn't want to argue with him over his daughters, and that appeared to be inevitable. If he would simply recognize his daughters' attempts to undermine their relationship, and *do* something about it, maybe things could work out. Whether that would happen one day appeared doubtful. Reid seemed to have so much of himself wrapped up in Terry and Jeanette that he never saw them in a true light. Maybe, she concluded, that's what it was like to love your own child—someone who is a separate human being but also a part of you.

Megan wiped a tear from the corner of her eye. Reid had suggested that they spend some time with Terry and Jeanette in a neutral place, somewhere that didn't provide constant reminders of the past. Megan couldn't see how a change of scenery would help. Being with the girls was going to be very difficult, especially in light of the fact that the wedding seemed to be indefinitely on hold. It would appear to Terry and Jeanette that they had won, at least temporarily. And hadn't they? Megan silently cursed herself for insisting that they not reschedule the ceremony right away. Deep down she hadn't expected

Reid to agree with her so readily. Maybe he was uncertain, too, and simply couldn't admit it.

As Megan stared up at the ceiling, she decided that she would give this upcoming weekend all she could. She would do her best to make friends with Terry and Jeanette and show them that their father would continue to love them and have time for them. A shudder passed through Megan as she admitted to herself that she wasn't sure her resolve was strong enough to handle another barrage of insults from the girls. And if she ever told the girls what she thought of them in front of Reid . . . well, it would all be over between them.

The ringing of the phone beside her bed startled Megan. Who could possibly be calling on a Sunday morning?

"Hello, Megan? This is Susan Parsons."

"Susan, hello! I didn't expect to hear from you again so soon. How are you?"

"Fine. My apologies for calling on a Sunday, but this couldn't wait. I want you to reconsider that assignment to Africa."

"You what?"

"After you turned it down, I lined up another writer, but he called yesterday to say he broke his arm on his kid's skateboard. Will you reconsider it? It would be such a great career move for you. I can't promise you anything, you understand, but this could lead to more."

"I don't know," Megan said doubtfully. "An awful lot has happened since we spoke last. I may be getting married."

"Well, congratulations! I had no idea. Who is the lucky man?"

"His name is Reid Spencer. He lives here in Boulder."

"I can see how that complicates things, but it needn't stand in your way. I could slip the schedule on the African article and put in one on New Zealand in its place. When's the wedding?"

"At the moment, I'm not sure. We had to postpone it, and . . . we haven't set a new date yet."

"Oh. I see. Well, if you could leave sometime next month, it would work out great for me."

"Next month? Susan, I don't see how I could leave a brand-new husband and fly off to Africa for a few months!"

"I don't know why not. Men travel in their work all the time. Before Hugh got sick, he traveled a great deal, didn't he? If it's okay for a man to do that, why isn't it okay for a woman? Honestly, Megan! You won't be giving up your writing after you marry, will you?"

"No. Of course not. Now, don't get on your soapbox," Megan said with a nervous laugh. "I agree in principle. I just don't think I could do that."

"Maybe you could postpone the wedding until after the assignment."

"No. That's out of the question." The thought flashed into her mind that the wedding might never be rescheduled, and what if that happened and she had also turned down the best career offer she was ever likely to get? Megan resolutely pushed such thoughts from her mind. She couldn't deal with them.

Susan sighed audibly. "Then you're saying no?"

"I don't know what to say. I want to do the article. I feel very strongly about the preservation of wild animals and keeping the savannas natural, but I have other considerations."

"I'm afraid you'll have to make up your mind. I hate to put you on the spot, but I have a production schedule to think about. What do you say?"

Megan let out her breath. "Count me out. It's a difficult decision, but I have to turn it down."

There was a long silence, and finally Susan said, "Well, I wish you the best. This must be quite a man for you to turn down something like this for him."

"He is."

"I guess that's it, then. I have to admit, I'm disappointed. I'd hoped that I could persuade you."

"In a way, I'm disappointed, too." Megan said goodbye and hung up the phone.

"Are you sure this is a good idea?" Megan asked as she crunched through the snow on her way to deposit their bags in the car. "It's only been two weeks. Maybe it's too soon."

"Of course it's a good idea. You and I can talk about this problem until we're blue in the face, and for days we have, but nothing is any different than it was. We need this weekend with the girls. This is the only way we'll ever get things worked out between you and them." Reid finished packing the food in the trunk, then added, "It'll be like a new start in a new place. Then Sunday, before we head back, we'll have a talk with them, explain how we feel and reason with them."

What could Megan say that she hadn't already said to Reid before? He insisted on trying to reason with his daughters as if they were his employees, and she instinctively knew that wouldn't work. But all she could do was go along with him and pray that she was wrong.

With a smile, Megan said, "I'm frankly surprised that Pamela agreed to let the girls come with us...but I'm pleased."

"Separate bedrooms. Remember I told you the travel agent booked us a cabin with three bedrooms. The girls will share one, and you and I will each have our own."

Megan looked at him in amusement. "We'll certainly be well chaperoned. But knowing you, if I had been in Pamela's place, I'm not sure I would have agreed."

"Even chaperones have to sleep sometime. When the girls doze off, I'll come to your room."

"See? What did I tell you? No way. My room is off-limits to you this weekend. This is going to be strictly platonic, just as you told their mother. I agree with her on this point."

"Yeah, I guess I do, too," he grumbled good-naturedly. "But I wish I didn't."

"You're not as lecherous as you pretend to be," she said with a smile. "Just almost." Megan wished that she felt as lighthearted as she pretended to be.

She got into the car and hoped Reid knew what he was doing. The whole idea still seemed precarious to her. Being fastened in a cabin with Terry and Jeanette all weekend was either going to get their relationship on the road to recovery or blow everything to bits. She had wanted to talk with Reid again before they picked up the girls, but the right words wouldn't form in her mind, and for some reason she was afraid to talk off the top of her head. As a writer, she was accustomed to being able to rework her words until she said exactly what she meant. This subject was too touchy to risk saying the wrong thing.

When they picked up the girls, Megan was again treated to a silhouette of Pamela, mourning in the doorway. The grief-stricken stance wasn't nearly as effective as it had been before, however, and Megan wondered if she were becoming callous.

As usual, the girls kept up a constant chatter with their father and ignored Megan altogether. The wedding fiasco wasn't mentioned, nor was Terry's health. Megan had decided that she should give the girls time with their father for a while without expecting to be included. If she had seemed to be a threat to the girls' attention from Reid, she could solve that by occupying herself with the sights of snowy fields and icy streams as they made their way up the mountains. On several occasions Reid spoke to Megan and she responded, but the girls initiated no conversation with her at all.

The cabin was new, privately owned by an out-of-state family who had used it only during the previous summer. Just off the cleared road in a copse of dense fir and spruce, its logs still had the honey-gold hue of fresh-cut timber.

Reid parked as close as he could, and they shouldered their suitcases and other paraphernalia for the short uphill climb.

"This is it?" Jeanette asked doubtfully. "I'll bet there's no TV."

"Yes, there is. The travel agent said so," replied Terry.

"Whose idea was this, anyway?" Jeanette asked. Terry cast a suspicious glance at Megan.

"It was your father's," Megan supplied.

"This is great!" Reid said enthusiastically. "I can almost smell the wood smoke already. After we get settled in, let's go for a long walk."

"A walk?" Terry stopped in her tracks on the porch steps. "Do I look like Smokey the Bear?"

Megan forced herself to smile at Terry as though she hadn't noticed that the comment was dripping with sarcasm. Grin and bear it, Megan. Make a friend. Don't be pushy. Megan's only consolation at the moment was that now that they were in the mountains, she was at least in her own element. Reid unlocked the door and held it for her while she entered. Megan took a deep breath of the cold air of the main room and tried to relax.

Cozy furniture was grouped around the native rock fireplace that dominated the far wall, and at the other end of the room was a trestle table and an open kitchen. While the cabin wasn't elaborate, Megan smiled her approval.

She crossed the room and opened the doors as Reid looked for the thermostat. There were two small bedrooms with twin beds, a bathroom between them, and to her left was a set of steps. After glancing up, Megan grinned. "I'll take this bedroom over here. You girls can have that one."

Reid looked around. "Only two bedrooms? The agent said there were three."

Megan pointed up, and he followed her finger. "An open loft? That's the third one?"

"Don't walk in your sleep," she counseled. "Maybe you should tie a rope around one foot, and tie the other end to the bed. Then if you fall over the edge, you won't go far."

"Funny. Very funny."

Megan laughed and deposited her bag in the bedroom she had chosen. "After all that riding, I for one am ready for a walk."

Reid rubbed his hands together in anticipation. "By the time we get back, the cabin should be warm."

"I don't want to go," Terry protested. "It's cold out there."

"It's cold in here, too. The walk will warm you up," Megan said.

"All right, I'll go. Dad says we have to do what you tell us to do, so I'll go. But I don't want to."

"Terry, if you'd rather stay here, maybe you should," Megan offered.

"No, Megan. The walk will be good for her. For all of us. On your feet, Terry."

Angrily Terry strode out with Jeanette at her heels. Reid looked at Megan reassuringly and said, "See? I told you things would be better."

Megan nodded as though she agreed, but she was less sure now than ever. With no other choice, Megan left the cabin and took the lead on their hike. To Megan's amazement, they had gone only a short distance before Jeanette was taking an interest in the snowy woods. Terry, however, predictably remained disgruntled. Noticing a few red berries, as bright against the snow as droplets of blood, Megan knelt and brushed the snow back from a kinnikinnick bush. As she examined the rounded green leaves, she said, "I'm surprised to find berries this late in the year."

"Are we supposed to eat them or something?" Jeanette asked.

"No. Indians sometimes use the leaves for tea or tobacco, but I don't think the berries are safe to eat."

Terry sighed to show her complete boredom.

"It's also called bearberry."

"There are bears around here?" Terry looked over her shoulder as she quickly moved closer to the others.

Megan hid her smile and led the way deeper into the woods. Around an outcropping of juniper they came upon a small herd of elk foraging in a clearing. The lead buck lifted his head and sniffed cautiously, but when no one moved, he went back to nibbling leaves from the bushes. Suddenly the wind shifted, and all the elk jerked their heads up. In a moment they had vanished into the protective cover of the brush.

"They're so pretty," Jeanette said with a sigh. "I've never seen elk so close."

"You sound like a Walt Disney movie," Terry said disparagingly.

"It was probably your perfume that chased them away," her sister retorted. "It smells like a bear."

"Now, Jeanette," Megan said with a laugh, "Terry's perfume isn't that strong."

"Go on and laugh at me!" Terry shouted at Megan. "You've never liked me!" She turned and flounced back toward the cabin. After a moment's hesitation, Jeanette ran after her.

"I wasn't laughing at her," Megan said helplessly. "You believe me, don't you?"

Reid's jaw was tightly clenched. "Of course," he snapped. "Terry's acting like a spoiled brat."

Megan looked up at him in surprise. "I didn t think you'd ever see that."

"I wasn't aware of this side of them until recently." Without another word, Reid started back for the cabin, and Megan quickly joined him. All the way back Megan wondered why Reid had emphasized the word *recently*. Did that mean he blamed her presence for his children's bad behavior? Surely not. Megan decided she'd better not try to conclude anything until Reid calmed down enough to discuss it.

When they got to the cabin, Reid began stacking a supply of logs on the porch for the fireplace. He didn't look any less upset, so Megan wordlessly helped him. From inside they could hear the raucous strains of a rock-music station.

"I guess they got back without being eaten by a bear," Reid observed dryly.

Seizing the opportunity to resume conversation, Megan quickly chimed in, "If I were a bear, I'd give Terry a wide berth." When Reid frowned at her, Megan laughingly said, "Well, you admitted she's a brat."

"No, I said she acts like one," he said carefully.

Exasperated, Megan let him finish stacking the wood alone. She went inside and knew at once that she had made a mistake. The cabin's serenity was shattered by the ear-splitting racket coming from the television. "Could you please turn that down?" she yelled over the din.

Both girls looked at her, then ignored her. When they paid no attention to her second request, without thinking, Megan reacted by unplugging the television set. Immediately both girls put up a howl.

"What's wrong?" Reid asked as he came in and looked from Megan to his daughters.

"She turned off the TV! And it was my favorite song," Jeanette wailed.

"Twice I asked them to turn it down, and they ignored me."

"Maybe they didn't hear you."

"They heard me."

"No, we didn't, Dad. Honest!" both girls protested as if on cue.

"Is it okay if they turn it back on now if they keep the sound turned down?" Reid suggested.

"That's not the point. They always ignore me, and I'm tired of their rudeness. The television stays off until after dinner."

"That seems a bit strict," Reid protested.

Megan saw the girls ranging behind him, and she knew much of her future relationship with them would depend on what happened next. "It's more important for them to learn manners than to listen to rock music."

Anger again flared in Reid's eyes, and for a minute Megan was afraid he would side against her. Finally he said, tightly, "You're right. You heard her, girls. No TV until after dinner." At once the girls began arguing with each other and throwing Megan lethal glances.

As Reid helped her cook dinner he said in an undertone, "That still seems harsh to me. Now they have nothing to do."

"Is that the way they treat their mother?" she whispered back.

"No, but she rarely gives them an ultimatum."

"Neither would I if they'd treat me like a human being."

Reid shredded the lettuce with unnecessary violence. "You make them sound like monsters."

"Try to put yourself in my place!"

"Have you tried to put yourself in theirs?" he countered.

"Dinner's ready," she snapped. "Come and eat."

The meal passed in frigid silence. Megan was so upset, she could hardly eat, but she was determined not to show any sign of weakness. As she forced bite after bite down her throat, she hoped she wouldn't throw up. She hadn't meant to blow up, but the tension had been unbearable, and it still was. As she swallowed another lump of food, she tried to resign herself to the fact that this weekend might well be her last with Reid Spencer.

Chapter Fifteen

As far as Megan was concerned, Saturday told the story of the rest of her life if she and Reid were to marry. So long as she and Reid were alone and refrained from talking about the girls, everything was wonderful. But the emotional climate when the girls were around was as frosty as the outdoors. Clearly, Reid would have to choose. The decision was his. If he married Megan, his relationship with his daughters might be irreparably damaged. And she knew that he was aware that she couldn't ultimately accept living with him and loving him without marriage. How Megan got through Saturday, she would never know.

By Sunday everyone's temper was frayed, and Megan desperately wished they could go home. Half a dozen times on Saturday she had almost suggested it but had stopped. If they had gone back to Boulder, Reid's visit with his daughters would have been cut short on her account, and he likely would not be able to see them again for two weeks, and then only if he moved into an apartment.

She watched the three of them playing Scrabble while she pretended to read. As long as she wasn't part of their activities, the girls were as open and loving as any she had ever seen. But she knew if she joined the game that both girls would become sullen and possessive of Reid. Megan enjoyed Scrabble, and it had been her idea to bring the game to the cabin, but she couldn't bring herself to intrude.

Resolutely she got up and put on her coat. "I'll be back. I'm going for a walk."

"Wait and I'll go with you," Reid said.

"No, no. You finish the game. I won't be long." She went out into the cold air and inhaled deeply, then let out a wreath of mist. After the strain of being unobtrusive, she was relieved to get away for a while.

She walked across the snowy yard and into the woods. She wasn't sure what she was looking for, but she wanted to find something of her own world to share with them. As Reid said, Terry and Jeanette didn't know her, not really. How could they be expected to like her if she did nothing more interesting than sit in the corner and read? She knew she was kidding herself to think that whatever she might do would change anything, but Megan was not a quitter. Hugh had called her "outright stubborn." Maybe he had been right. Megan couldn't and wouldn't give up.

Along with frustration over not being able to win the girls' affection, Megan was wrestling with her struggle to simply be accepted. She honestly wasn't jealous of the place the girls held in Reid's heart—certainly she wouldn't want to change that. At the same time, she wondered why it was so very difficult to be a part of their family. Did all stepparents go through this? She didn't want to take Pamela's place, but she wanted very much to have a place of her own. Worst of all, Terry and Jeanette's continued mistreatment of her was threatening to come between Reid and herself.

Tears stung her eyes, and she brushed them away angrily. All her life Megan had hated to cry. She couldn't do it prettily like Pamela, and it always gave her a headache. Nevertheless, the tears gathered and spilled over, and as she sat alone on a fallen log, she gave in to her sadness. It seemed a long while before she felt drained enough to quit crying. She leaned her head back against the rough bark of a tree and drew a deep breath, hoping to regain her composure. She was afraid her face would still be blotchy when she returned, and they would all know she'd cried. Already she felt a dull throb behind her eyes.

As she sat waiting for her courage to return, she noticed the snow was dotted with fir cones about as long as her finger. With a sigh, Megan got up and began gathering them. Pinecones weren't much to show for her walk, but otherwise someone might guess she had been out here crying. Megan picked up as many cones as she could carry. As she was about to start back, she heard a rustling sound in the woods farther along the way. She paused to listen, but the woods were silent again.

With a shrug, she moved away from the log and back toward the cabin.

Again she heard the rustling and what sounded like a muffled cough. Megan turned. "Reid? Is that you?"

In the distance she heard the call of a bird but nothing else. She frowned. She was well out of sight of the cabin, and as far as she knew, there were no other people around.

She resumed walking but once more heard the sound of something or someone behind her. Could Terry or Jeanette have come out to try to frighten her? Nothing else seemed likely, so she lifted her chin stubbornly and ignored the noises.

By the time she reached the cabin the sounds she'd been hearing were far enough behind her to be of no concern. If the girls had expected to alarm her, they would be sadly mistaken.

Megan stamped the snow from her feet and shouldered open the door. Reid and the girls were just finishing their game. Megan paused and looked back toward the woods. What had she heard?

"Close the door," Terry complained. "You're letting the cold in."

Megan kicked it shut and carried the armload of cones to the hearth. "Let's make fire flowers."

"What?" Jeanette looked at her with interest as Terry slumped lower in her chair.

"When you burn pinecones, they make fire flowers and glow like neon. Go get another log, and I'll show you."

Jeanette pulled on her coat as Reid came to kneel on the hearth beside Megan. "You were gone a long time," he said softly. "I was getting worried." He touched her face gently. "Your nose is red."

"It's cold outside."

"When are we going home?" Terry asked with excessive boredom.

"As soon as this last log burns," Megan replied. "I wanted to show you this first."

Terry closed her eyes and looked as if she were going to sleep.

"I want to get to know you," Megan told the girl with sincerity, "and I want you to know me."

"You expect burning a bunch of pinecones will do that?"

Reid frowned at her before he said to Megan, "It seems to be taking Jeanette a long time to get that log."

"I guess she had to go all the way to the woodpile." Megan stood and went to look out the kitchen window.

Jeanette was crouching beside the woodpile, peering over the top at a large bear that was snuffling at her tracks only a short distance away.

Megan's heart leaped into her throat as she realized what the rustling sounds behind her had been and the danger Jeanette was in now. Grabbing two pots from the kitchen cabinet, she ran out the door, loudly banging the pots together and shouting at the top of her lungs.

The bear grunted in surprise and rose on his hind legs. But his instinct to flee overcame his impulse to attack. With a ripple of fur and muscle, he ran back to the safety of the woods.

Megan threw down the pots and raced to Jeanette. "Are you all right?" she demanded anxiously.

Jeanette threw her arms around Megan and sobbed brokenly on her shoulder. "I couldn't get back to the house! I thought the bear was going to get me! I was afraid to scream!"

"Hush, hush. It's all right now. He's gone. See?"

Jeanette still clung to her in desperation. "You saved my life!"

"Come back to the cabin."

By this time Reid had reached them, and he put his arm protectively around them both as he stared after the bear.

Megan's knees felt weak as she thought what a near catastrophe they had had. At this time of the year bears had little food and were aggressive. This one was probably accustomed to raiding the cabin's garbage, for he had shown no fear at all of being close to the house and people. Other tenants might even have encouraged him by tossing him scraps.

"How did you know that you could frighten him away?" Jeanette asked tearfully.

"I didn't."

"And you ran out anyway?"

Megan bent to pick up the pans. One was badly dented. "You may lose some of your deposit, Reid."

Terry was waiting for them on the porch, her arms wrapped around her against the cold. "It's all your fault!" she yelled at Megan. "You were out here. I'll bet you knew the bear was out here, and you sent Jeanette after wood!"

"I did not!" Megan gasped in horror.

"You probably did it so you could save her life and look like a big deal to Dad!"

Anger burst inside Megan, and this time she couldn't repress it. "That is the most stupid thing I've ever heard!" She took the steps two at a time and backed Terry into the house as she shook her finger under the girl's nose. "I've put up with a lot from you, but this does it! Do you honestly think I would endanger either of you for any reason whatsoever?"

"My mom says—"

"Your mother is causing trouble in this family, and you're plenty old enough to recognize it!"

"Don't you dare talk about Mom like that!" Terry shrieked.

"Both of you calm down!" Reid roared.

Megan wheeled on him. "I will not be corrected as if I were a child! If you want to change anyone's behavior, then change theirs. These are the worst-behaved kids I've ever seen!"

Jeanette began to wail and Terry to shout as Reid and Megan glared at each other. "Look at this!" Megan demanded. "Who do you think caused it? Me?"

"If you'll just—"

In no mood to listen to anything, Megan continued her angry outburst. "If I'll just what? Is it all right for Terry to run me down? For Jeanette to pretend she can't see me or hear me? What about my rights?" Turning on her heel, she ran to her bedroom, slammed the door behind her and began throwing her things into her suitcase. All the while she grumbled under her breath and threatened all manner of things that she didn't truly mean.

Her tears were flowing again, and she wiped them away with the palm of her hand. At this point she was too upset to care if anyone saw her cry. She wondered what was going on between Reid and his daughters. Was he commiserating with them on what a mistake he had almost made with her? Had her burst of anger driven him away forever?

Megan sat on the edge of her bed and buried her face in her hands. In the next room she could hear their raised voices but could not make out their words. A sick knot tightened in her stomach. Because of the things she'd said in anger she might have alienated the most important person in her life. Even though she was angry at him for not defending her, she still loved him. Above all, she loved him.

Megan straightened and forced herself to stop crying. If he was this easily lost, then he wasn't in love with her anyway, she reasoned. She couldn't live the rest of her life alienated from him whenever his daughters were around.

Taking a deep breath, Megan lifted her suitcase and went into the main room, not knowing what to expect. Reid was furious. She could tell that at a glance. Not allowing herself to quail, Megan started for the door. "I'll wait for you in the car," she said in a clipped tone.

"No. I want you to hear this." Reid took the suitcase from her and tossed it onto the couch. Turning back to the girls he said, "I've had it from you two. Ever since Megan came into my life, you've acted like spoiled, selfish brats. I've put up with it because I thought the three of you could work it out. I've put up with it and risked losing the woman I love because I hoped you'd change. I was wrong to do that."

He reached out and pulled Megan to his side. Pointing at her, he said, "I love this woman. She's a part of my life, and she will be from now on. She won't go away just because you act like...snippish churls." He turned to Megan. "Isn't that right?"

"Yes, Reid," she said in surprise. "I won't leave you for any reason."

"And I won't leave you. People who love each other don't fold up and run away when the going gets rough." He pointed his accusing finger at each girl in turn. "And for damn sure they don't let children dictate how their lives will be run. Now, you two have a choice to make. You must show Megan respect, and I won't have anything to do with you until you do. You've put me in the position of having to make a choice, and I choose Megan. I want you and I love you but not the same way I love her."

Megan's eyes filled again, and she stared at Reid in amazement. When he cleared the air he didn't fool around.

"As for your mother being a troublemaker, it's true and you both know it. I've seen Megan put up with more than any woman should have to, and I won't stand for it any longer. Jeanette, stop that sniveling! Terry, get that look off your face or I'll turn you over my knee! Now, both of you, get packed."

The girls broke and ran as if they thought he might leave without them.

"As for you," he continued to Megan, "I've had all I'm going to take from you, too. I love you, and you love me. We're getting married, and that's final!"

"When?"

"Tomorrow! And if that preacher can't or won't marry us, we'll go to every church in town until we find one who will. You want a church wedding, and you're going to have one if we have to drive all the way to Denver to get it!" He paused as if he thought he might have gone too far and glared at her.

Megan threw her arms around his neck and buried her face against his throat. "I love you," she sobbed. "I love you so damn much!"

Reid held her tightly, and she felt him tremble. "We came close to losing it, didn't we?" he whispered solemnly.

She shook her head. "Not our love. We won't ever lose that." Pulling back she said, "Did you mean everything you said? What if they choose not to see you if I'm still around?"

"If they love me, they'll see me. And you. And it won't be like an armed camp. I won't stand for them acting like this."

"I shouldn't have said that about Pamela," she admitted.

"It's true. I suspect they would have come around long before this if Pamela hadn't encouraged them to be so rude to you."

Megan smiled faintly. "'Snippish churls?'"

"I was mad, but there's a limit to what a man can say in front of his daughters."

"I think you handled it quite well."

"Megan, you weren't going to leave me, were you? I couldn't stand it if I thought you were."

"I was afraid you were going to leave me. No, I'm not going anywhere. Not unless it's with you."

"And that's another thing. We're having our honeymoon right away—we're leaving for Europe on Tuesday, if we have to go by barge!"

"I love you."

"You're even beautiful when you cry," he said softly.

"I guess love really is blind," she said as she laughed through her tears.

He gently brushed the dampness from her cheeks. "The only reason I ever want you to cry is for happiness."

"I am."

Once again Megan put on her wedding dress. The cleaners had done a good job of removing the mud stains from the hem, and the dress looked like new. As Reid zipped it up, Megan had a sensation of déjà vu, and it wasn't a pleasant experience.

Since they had dropped Terry and Jeanette off at their house the day before, the girls had not once called. Pamela had, however, and judging from Reid's end of the conversation, Megan wondered if things might be worse than ever.

"Quit worrying," he said as he put his arms around her.

"I can't help it. I was thinking about Jeanette and Terry."

"They're old enough to take responsibility for their own actions. This is our wedding day. All I want you to think of is how happy we'll be."

She smiled up at him. "I don't have any doubts about that."

"When you smile at me with that certain smile of yours, your whole face seems to light up."

"I'm happy with you. This smile is just for you and nobody else."

"Get your coat or we'll be late." He kissed her forehead.

Megan glanced out the window. "At least the sun is shining this time. Maybe our luck will change."

"I thought you said it was good luck for it to rain on the wedding day."

"Well, that probably is true somewhere."

They drove to the church and again parked in the covered drive. "We have it all to ourselves today," Megan commented. "I guess Monday afternoon isn't a popular time to get married."

"This was the only time the preacher had free. I see Chad's car over there. At least we have a best man."

They went into the chapel and were met by the preacher and Chad. The organist began playing softly. She was to be their other witness.

Chad greeted them both and asked, "How are the girls?"

"Fine," Reid said without elaborating.

"Shouldn't we wait for them?"

"No. They won't be here."

Chad looked surprised but covered it quickly. "In that case, I guess we're ready."

Reid and Megan gave him the rings. Together they went down to the altar.

Megan put her hand in Reid's and noticed his fingers were as cold as her own. He might have said he didn't care that his daughters weren't there, but Megan knew he was deeply hurt. They had had ample time to get home from school and come to the church.

"Dearly beloved," the preacher began.

Suddenly there was the sound of a door opening and shutting. Everyone turned to look toward the rear of the chapel. Terry and Jeanette stood there in their rose-colored dresses. Jeanette wore the string of coral beads that Megan had bought for her, and she was smiling tremulously.

Megan and Reid stared at the girls as they came down the short aisle. "Traffic held us up," Terry said.

"You can't get married without attendants," Jeanette explained. Terry frowned and rolled her eyes toward the ceiling as if she found it far more interesting than anything happening at the altar rail. Jeanette jabbed her sharply with her elbow and smiled at Megan and Reid.

Megan's eyes met Reid's, and she raised her eyebrows as her lips curved up. They both knew the girls hadn't changed overnight, but they also knew this was a beginning, a very important beginning for them all. The preacher began once more, and Megan knew that this time there would be nothing to stand in the way of their happiness.

* * * * *

HEATHER GRAHAM POZZESSERE
Shadows on the Nile

CHAPTER ONE

Alex could tell that the woman was very nervous. Her fingers were wound tightly about the arm rests, and she had been staring straight ahead since the flight began. Who was she? Why was she flying alone? Why to Egypt? She was a small woman, fine-boned, with classical features and porcelain skin. Her hair was golden blond, and she had blue-gray eyes that were slightly tilted at the corners, giving her a sensual and exotic appeal.

And she smelled divine. He had been sitting there, glancing through the flight magazine, and her scent had reached him, filling him like something rushing through his bloodstream, and before he had looked at her he had known that she would be beautiful.

John was frowning at him. His gaze clearly said that this was not the time for Alex to become interested in a woman. Alex lowered his head, grinning. Nuts to John. He was the one who had made the reservations so late that there was already another passenger between them in their row. Alex couldn't have remained silent anyway; he was certain that he could ease the flight for her. Besides, he had to know her name, had to see if her eyes would turn silver when she smiled. Even though he should, he couldn't ignore her.

"Alex," John said warningly.

Maybe John was wrong, Alex thought. Maybe this was precisely the right time for him to get involved. A woman would be the perfect shield, in case anyone was interested in his business in Cairo.

The two men should have been sitting next to each other, Jillian decided. She didn't know why she had wound up sandwiched between the two of them, but she couldn't do a thing about it. Frankly, she was far too nervous to do much of anything.

"It's really not so bad," a voice said sympathetically. It came from her right. It was the younger of the two men, the one next to the window. "How about a drink? That might help."

Jillian took a deep, steadying breath, then managed to answer. "Yes . . . please. Thank you."

His fingers curled over hers. Long, very strong fingers, nicely tanned. She had noticed him when she had taken her seat—he was difficult not to notice. There was an arresting quality about him. He had a certain look: high-powered, confident, self-reliant. He was medium tall and medium built, with shoulders that nicely filled out his suit jacket, dark brown eyes, and sandy hair that seemed to defy any effort at combing it. And he had a wonderful voice, deep and compelling. It broke through her fear and actually soothed her. Or perhaps it was the warmth of his hand over hers that did it.

"Your first trip to Egypt?" he asked. She managed a brief nod, but was saved from having to comment when the stewardess came by. Her companion ordered her a white wine, then began to converse with her quite normally, as if unaware that her fear of flying had nearly rendered her speechless. He asked her what she did for a living, and she heard herself tell him that she was a music teacher at a junior college. He responded easily to everything she said, his voice warm and concerned each time he asked another question. She didn't think; she simply answered him, because flying had become easier the moment he touched her. She even told him that she was a widow, that her husband had been killed in a car accident four years ago, and that she was here now to fulfill a long-held dream, because she had always longed to see the pyramids, the Nile and all the ancient wonders Egypt held.

She had loved her husband, Alex thought, watching as pain briefly darkened her eyes. Her voice held a thread of sadness when she mentioned her husband's name. Out of nowhere, he wondered how it would feel to be loved by such a woman.

Alex noticed that even John was listening, commenting on things now and then. How interesting, Alex thought, looking across at his friend and associate.

The stewardess came with the wine. Alex took it for her, chatting casually with the woman as he paid. Charmer, Jillian thought ruefully. She flushed, realizing that it was his charm that had led her to tell him so much about her life.

Her fingers trembled when she took the wineglass. "I'm sorry," she murmured. "I don't really like to fly."

Alex—he had introduced himself as Alex, but without telling her his last name—laughed and said that was the understatement of the year. He pointed out the window to the clear blue sky—an omen of good things to come, he said—then assured her that the airline had an excellent safety record. His friend, the older man with the haggard, world-weary face, eventually introduced himself as John. He joked and tried to reassure her, too, and eventually their efforts paid off. Once she felt a little calmer, she offered to move, so they could converse without her in the way.

Alex tightened his fingers around hers, and she felt the startling warmth in his eyes. His gaze was appreciative and sensual, without being insulting. She felt a rush of sweet heat swirl within her, and she realized with surprise that it was excitement, that she was enjoying his company the way a woman enjoyed the company of a man who attracted her. She had thought she would never feel that way again.

"I wouldn't move for all the gold in ancient Egypt," he said with a grin, "and I doubt that John would, either." He touched her cheek. "I might lose track of you, and I don't even know your name."

"Jillian," she said, meeting his eyes. "Jillian Jacoby."

He repeated her name softly, as if to commit it to memory, then went on to talk about Cairo, the pyramids at Giza, the Valley of the Kings, and the beauty of the nights when the sun set over the desert in a riot of blazing red.

And then the plane was landing. To her amazement, the flight had ended. Once she was on solid ground again, Jillian realized that Alex knew all sorts of things about her, while she didn't know a thing about him or John— not even their full names.

They went through customs together. Jillian was immediately fascinated, in love with the colorful atmosphere of Cairo, and not at all dismayed by the waiting and the bureaucracy. When they finally reached the street she fell head over heels in love with the exotic land. The heat shimmered in the air, and taxi drivers in long burnooses lined up for fares. She could hear the soft singsong of their language, and she was thrilled to realize that the dream she had harbored for so long was finally coming true.

She didn't realize that two men had followed them from the airport to the street. Alex, however, did. He saw the men behind him, and his jaw tightened as he nodded to John to stay put and hurried after Jillian.

"Where are you staying?" he asked her.

"The Hilton," she told him, pleased at his interest. Maybe her dream was going to turn out to have some unexpected aspects.

He whistled for a taxi. Then, as the driver opened the door, Jillian looked up to find Alex staring at her. She felt...something. A fleeting magic raced along her spine, as if she knew what he was about to do. Knew, and should have protested, but couldn't.

Alex slipped his arm around her. One hand fell to her waist, the other cupped her nape, and he kissed her. His mouth was hot, his touch firm, persuasive. She was filled with heat; she trembled...and then she broke away at last, staring at him, the look in her eyes more eloquent than any words. Confused, she turned away and stepped into the taxi. As soon as she was seated she turned to stare after him, but he was already gone, a part of the crowd.

She touched her lips as the taxi sped toward the heart of the city. She shouldn't have allowed the kiss; she barely knew him. But she couldn't forget him.

She was still thinking about him when she reached the Hilton. She checked in quickly, but she was too late to acquire a guide for the day. The manager suggested that she stop by the Kahil bazaar, not far from the hotel. She dropped her bags in her room, then took another taxi to the bazaar. Once again she was enchanted. She loved everything: the noise, the people, the donkey carts that blocked the narrow streets, the shops with their beaded entryways and beautiful wares in silver and stone, copper and brass. Old men smoking water pipes sat on mats drinking tea, while younger men shouted out their wares from stalls and doorways. Jillian began walking slowly, trying to take it all in. She was occasionally jostled, but she kept her hand on her purse and sidestepped quickly. She was just congratulating herself on her competence when she was suddenly dragged into an alley by two Arabs swaddled in burnooses.

"What—" she gasped, but then her voice suddenly fled. The alley was empty and shadowed, and night was coming. One man had a scar on his cheek, and held a long, curved knife; the other carried a switchblade.

"Where is it?" the first demanded.

"Where is what?" she asked frantically.

The one with the scar compressed his lips grimly. He set his knife against her cheek, then stroked the flat side down to her throat. She could feel the deadly coolness of the steel blade.

"Where is it? Tell me now!"

Her knees were trembling, and she tried to find the breath to speak. Suddenly she noticed a shadow emerging from the darkness behind her attackers. She gasped, stunned, as the man drew nearer. It was Alex.

Alex...silent, stealthy, his features taut and grim. Her heart seemed to stop. Had he come to her rescue? Or was he allied with her attackers, there to threaten, even destroy, her?

* * * * *

Watch for Chapter Two of SHADOWS ON THE NILE coming next month—only in Silhouette Intimate Moments.

Silhouette Special Edition

COMING NEXT MONTH

#415 TIME AFTER TIME—Billie Green
Airline executives Leah French and Paul Gregory had a cool, professional relationship. Then the dreams began, dreams that carried them out of time, to faraway lands and into each other's arms.

#416 FOOLS RUSH IN—Ginna Gray
In tracing her missing twin, Erin Blaine's first find was dashing Max Delany, her sister's supposed beloved. Dodging gunmen and double-crossers, Max and Erin sought clues...and stumbled onto unwanted desire.

#417 WHITE NIGHTS—Dee Norman
Whether racing down ski slopes or chasing the chills in a hot tub, Jennifer Ericson couldn't seem to avoid hostile financier Travis MacKay. Though he suspected her of pursuing him, she was really only running from love.

#418 TORN ASUNDER—Celeste Hamilton
Years ago Alexa Thorpe, the boss's daughter, and Ty Duncan, the laborer's son, fell in forbidden love, but family objections and deceptions drove them apart. By tackling their history, could they succeed in sharing a future?

#419 SUMMER RAIN—Lisa Jackson
Widowed Ainsley Hughes reluctantly brought her troubled son to her father's ranch, only to find the Circle S failing...and aloof Trent McCullough in charge. She'd once loved Trent's fire, but could she trust his iciness now?

#420 LESSONS IN LOVING—Bay Matthews
Bachelor Mitch Bishop had much to learn about parenting, and special ed teacher Jamie Carr was the perfect instructor. But in the school of love, both adults faltered on their ABC's.

AVAILABLE THIS MONTH